"Why are they all looking at me?" Perrie asked, taking a gulp of champagne.

Joe leaned back in his chair. "They want to dance with you, but they think you're with me."

The bubbles from the champagne went down the wrong way and she coughed. "Am—am I with you, Brennan?" she asked, her eyes watering.

He gazed into her eyes for a long time, his devilish smile sending her back for more champagne. "Yeah, you are. Do you want to dance?"

Perrie nodded. The dance floor was crowded, but Joe found them a small spot and pulled her close. Emboldened by the champagne, Perrie wrapped her arms around his neck and pressed her hips into his, nuzzling her face into the soft flannel of his shirt. *Why was there always flannel between them? Why couldn't she and Joe have met on a tropical island where the men barely wore clothes?*

The music stopped. Perrie risked a look up at Joe, and their gazes locked. The smoldering passion in his eyes caused her heart to lurch. He pulled her body tight against his and his desire, hard and hot, branded her flesh through her jeans.

"So what's going to happen tonight, Perrie?"

Dear Reader,

It seemed like a good plan. Three bachelors setting off for the Alaskan bush to start a new life, far away from the female sex. But then Bachelor #1, Tanner O'Neill, got an early Christmas present in the person of beautiful Julia Logan in my December 1997 release, *Caught Under the Mistletoe!*

Now Valentine's Day is upon us and Bachelor #2, bush pilot Joe Brennan, is in serious danger of following his best buddy to the altar. Finding women for these three boys has been a real treat, and I think you'll enjoy watching Joe as he's *Dodging Cupid's Arrow!*— and ducking his desire for investigative reporter Perrie Kincaid.

And then get ready for my last bachelor to be *Struck by Spring Fever!* in April 1998. Wilderness guide Kyle "Hawk" Hawkins has a lady waiting to capture his heart and warm his bed after a long, cold Alaskan winter!

Happy Valentine's Day,

Kate Hoffmann

P.S. I love to hear from my readers. Write to me: c/o Harlequin Books, 225 Duncan Mill Road, Don Mills, Ontario, Canada, M3B 3K9

DODGING CUPID'S ARROW!
Kate Hoffmann

Harlequin Books

TORONTO • NEW YORK • LONDON
AMSTERDAM • PARIS • SYDNEY • HAMBURG
STOCKHOLM • ATHENS • TOKYO • MILAN
MADRID • WARSAW • BUDAPEST • AUCKLAND

With special thanks to Wally Kohler,
for answering my endless questions about pilots
and their planes.

ISBN 0-373-25770-8

DODGING CUPID'S ARROW!

_____Prologue_____

Five years ago

JOE BRENNAN HELD his breath as the rough plank door swung open, its hinges groaning in protest. If the interior of Bachelor Creek Lodge looked anything like the exterior, he vowed he would turn around and head right back to Seattle.

"I should have my head examined," he murmured to himself, his gaze scanning the dilapidated log building. He sidestepped a rotted board on the porch, then squinted into a dust-coated window. A shaft of light illuminated the interior and his gaze followed it up to a huge hole in the roof.

"Look at this," Hawk said, pointing to the log lintel above the front door. Joe and Tanner glanced up. No Wimin Kin Pass was crudely carved into the wood.

"I'm not sure there's a woman on this planet who would willingly set foot inside this place," Joe said.

He never should have let Tanner O'Neill talk him into this harebrained scheme. He and the third in their trio, Kyle Hawkins, had left everything behind—their careers, their homes...females—to move to the wilds of Alaska and start a business.

Tanner's inheritance looked good on paper. A wilderness lodge a mile from the tiny bush town of Muleshoe, land right on the Yukon River with their very own creek running just outside the back door. But the photos didn't do justice to the wreck of a lodge. Had they been more accurate, Joe might have opted to stay home.

In Seattle, he'd had a good job, a partnership in a small law firm with a generous salary. A few weekends a month, he would fly for the Army Reserve, putting a long-held pilot's license to use. He filled the rest of his life with sports and women, two of his favorite pastimes. Life was good and he had been happy.

He knew he'd be giving up more than he could even imagine to move to Alaska. But the plan had been too tempting to resist. Tanner would run the lodge, or what was left of it, and Hawk would serve as a wilderness guide for their clients, once they had them. And Joe would pilot their plane, a De Havilland Otter that the three of them had bought on a shoestring budget. He would ferry clients and supplies from Fairbanks to Muleshoe, landing on the tiny airstrip as he and Hawk and Tanner had done just minutes before.

"Don't be too quick to judge," Tanner warned as he stepped through the door. "Try to think of the potential."

Joe turned to give Hawk a dubious look. "With all this potential, I think we're going to need to buy a bigger plane. Something that might carry a bulldozer." His friend's expression was unreadable but Joe suspected he was harboring some of the same concerns. If the lodge's exterior was any clue, the interior was probably uninhabitable, which left the three of them essentially homeless. Until Tanner's carpentry skills could be proved, they might as well pitch a tent. "Let's see how bad it is," he muttered, crossing the threshold.

Dust motes drifted in the shaft of sunlight that streamed through the hole in the roof. A ragged collection of hand-hewn furniture lay scattered around the room, bits of stuffing littering the floor. A huge moose head stared down at them from above the stone fireplace, as if mocking their high expectations.

"It's not so bad," Tanner said, slowly taking in the disrepair. "Once the roof is patched and we've cleaned up a bit, it will be just fine."

"Fine for raccoons and other wildlife," Joe replied. "We've barely got a roof over our head, O'Neill. And you forget that the nights here are a lot colder than in Seattle."

"Come on, Brennan, where's your sense of adventure?" Tanner teased. "So we'll be roughing it for a while. Suck it up and be a man."

Joe shook his head. "I guess I can always sleep in the cabin of the Otter."

"Or under the stars," Hawk said, distracted by his survey of the hearth. He looked up into the chimney. "Squirrels," was his only comment.

Joe considered his friend's suggestion. For Hawk, sleeping in the wild was no great hardship. In fact, Joe suspected his friend would revel in the rustic living conditions. Hawk would no longer have to leave home to get a wilderness fix as he had done in Seattle, sometimes disappearing for two or three weeks without a word. His buddy was always up for an adventure, the more challenging and spontaneous, the better.

Tanner finished his survey of the interior, then looked at his friends. "I know this isn't what you expected," he said. "And I guess if either of you wants to bail, now's the time to say so." He paused, then hitched his hands on his waist. "But before you make your decision, I want you to know that I'm determined to make this work— with or without you."

Silence hung in the dusty air for a long moment. Then Hawk shrugged. "I'm still in," he said. He looked at Joe and the challenge was evident in his gaze. A good buddy would stick it out, and the three of them were the best of buddies. And at this point, there wasn't much left for Joe in Seattle besides a handful of disappointed women and a storage locker full of his belongings.

Joe raked his fingers through his hair. What the hell was he doing? One look at the tiny bush town of Muleshoe was enough to see that there wasn't much social life in the outback of Alaska. It wasn't as if he couldn't live without women, but he did have certain needs.

"What'll it be, Brennan? In or out?"

Joe turned to Tanner. "I can see us fifty years from now. Three toothless old bachelors reminiscing about the good old days in Seattle. Remembering the last time we laid eyes on a beautiful woman."

"There are beautiful women in Alaska," Tanner said. "They're just spread out over a bigger geographical area. You have to go find 'em."

Joe took a final glance around the lodge, then winced. "I swear I must be crazy. But if you guys are staying, then so am I."

Tanner clapped his hand on Joe's back and laughed. "I knew you couldn't resist. In all the time I've known you, you've never backed away from a challenge."

"This is one time I really wish I was more of a wimp," Joe said, shaking his head. He held out his hand. Tanner placed his palm over it, then Hawk did the same.

"To the boys of Bachelor Creek Lodge," Tanner said.

"Bachelor Creek," Hawk repeated.

"I think we've all gone crazy," Joe said, wondering why he was always drawn into impossible situations.

He suspected it was a character flaw, though he wasn't really sure. But stuck in the Alaskan wilderness, facing a future full of challenges, he knew it wouldn't take long to find out.

1

"ONE OF THESE DAYS, I really should have my head examined."

Joe leaned forward and scraped at the frost-coated windshield of his Super Cub. His gaze caught the air temperature gauge, a nagging reminder of an ever present danger. The outside temperature was forty degrees below zero and his defroster had reached its limit. If he flew much higher, he'd be flying blind. Or the engine would quit from the cold and he wouldn't be flying at all.

He peered through the windshield at the craggy ridges below, so sheer not even snow clung to the rock. Denali. "The High One," as the native Athabascans had named it. Mount McKinley was the highest peak in North America and a magnet for climbers worldwide. And buzzing back and forth between Talkeetna and the mountain were the Denali fliers, those pilots who ferried climbers and gear to "Kahiltna International," the name given to the glacier at the bottom of the climbing route.

Since Joe had arrived in Alaska five years before, he'd heard tale after tale of their exploits—risky landings and daring rescues, true artists behind the controls of their airplanes. He'd grudgingly admired them, until he'd been accepted into the fold. After that, he'd held them in even greater awe.

His initiation had been achieved more by default than

daring. He'd been flying a client over "the Hill" on a sight-seeing trip when he'd noticed a spot of color near the edge of the Kahiltna Glacier near Denali's base. He dropped low then circled, his curiosity piqued. What he found had sent a chill through his blood. A Cessna, flipped upside down, the white belly of the plane barely visible against the snow. If he hadn't been looking in that exact spot, he would have missed it, along with countless other pilots flying in the area.

With the approval of his adventure-hungry passenger, he put his own plane down near the crash site, then struggled through the crusty snow to the overturned plane. The two of them had dragged three injured passengers and the unconscious pilot from the Cessna. And later, when more help had been summoned and all had been evacuated to the hospital in Anchorage, he'd been credited with saving the life of one of Denali's favorite fliers, Skip Christiansen, and given honorary membership in the elite fraternity. They'd nicknamed him Eagle Eyes Brennan.

Skip had talked him into this current mess—searching for a stranded Swedish climber who'd attempted a solo winter ascent of Denali. Skip had flown the woman in a week before and now had been charged with coordinating an air search to aid the park rangers. Six planes swept along the climbing route, each one required to descend out of the thinner air for a time after each run for safety's sake.

Had Joe been safe at home in Muleshoe rather than hanging out in a Talkeetna watering hole, trying to charm a beautiful girl into spending the evening with him, he would never have been drawn into the search, flying too high, too cold, breathing bottled oxygen every now and then to keep his head clear.

But Joe Brennan was never one to shrink from a challenge. And flying at the far edge of his talents and near the mechanical limitations of his plane was exactly the adrenaline rush he'd come to crave. Still, that didn't mean that he couldn't question his good sense once he was caught up in another risky venture.

"All right, Brennan," he muttered to himself. "Let's reevaluate your escape plan."

Although Joe was considered a gutsy flyer by his Denali pals, he tempered that characteristic with a good dose of self-preservation. No matter where he flew, over ice or rock, forest or mountain, he always had a contingency plan, a way out if oil pressure dropped or his engine failed.

He spotted a small saddle of clear snow to the north and fixed it in his mind. If worse came to worse, he could put the Cub down there, landing uphill to slow the plane, then turning around to take off downhill. An air current, swirling near the sheer rock face, buffeted the Cub and Joe cursed.

"A solo ascent in the middle of an Alaskan winter," he muttered. "Now, there's a great idea, lady. Why not just jump into a crevasse and get it over with?"

The truth be told, he couldn't begrudge the climber her passion for a new challenge. Since he'd started flying in the bush, he'd accepted one dangerous job after another, always cognizant of his limitations but never afraid to push a little harder. He'd landed on glaciers and sandbars, lakes and landing strips in all conditions, in weather not fit for flying. And he'd loved it all.

He scratched another patch of ice off the windshield. "Come on, sweetheart. Show me where you are. Point the way." He pushed his sunglasses up on his head and scanned the area. Though he was slightly west of the usual route to the summit, he knew that a climber could easily become confused from the altitude or exhaustion.

One misstep was all it took and hypoxia would take over, dulling the senses until frostbite and hypothermia set in. Without a partner to take up the slack, a solo ascent was a ticket to trouble. Before long, a climber would sit down in the snow, unable to move, unable to think. That's when either death or the Denali fliers moved in, snatching half-frozen climbers off the face of the mountain and bringing them back to safety.

Wispy clouds surrounded the plane for a moment and Joe scratched the ice off his side window. "I don't need weather," he muttered at the approaching cloud bank. He dropped lower, beneath the cloud level, heading back down the mountain. The head of the Kahiltna Glacier passed below him now, safe landing and breathable air at eleven thousand feet. Suddenly, a flash of color glittered from an ice face in front of him. He stared at the spot lower on the glacier, squinting to make out a bright blue scrap of nylon.

As he descended on the glacier, the patch of blue became a pack, half-buried in the snow. He looked closer and thought he saw a rope tracing a path into the shadow of a deep crevasse.

Joe snatched up his radio. "Denali Rescue, this is Piper three-six-three-nine Delta Tango. I think I have her. She's well west of the usual route on the lower part of the glacier. It looks like she fell into a crevasse. She was roped, but I don't see her. Over."

The radio crackled and he recognized Skip's voice. "Three-nine Delta, this is seven-four Foxtrot. Good eyes! I'm just off your left wing. I'll go down and search until Park Rescue arrives. Over."

"I found her, Skip, I'm going down."

"Buddy, that's a tricky landing. You catch a ski and you're done, never mind negotiating those crevasses. I took her in, I'll get her out."

"You just back me up. I'm heading down. Three-nine Delta, out."

Joe banked to the east, drawing a lazy circle around the stranded climber. Time after time, he passed over the ice field, flying from bottom to top as he judged the surface, memorizing every bump and hole in the ice. His pulse pounded in his head as he descended, his eyes fixed on a point above him on the mountain. An instant later, he felt the skis shudder and he cut the power. Slowly, the plane climbed the face of the glacier until it would go no further. Then he maneuvered it around until it faced down the slope, ready to take off in the same tracks he'd landed in.

Not two hundred feet below him, he saw the rope. Joe yanked the flap on his hood over his face and adjusted his sunglasses, then pushed against the door with his shoulder. He wasn't sure what he would find, but he hoped for the best.

He grabbed a canister of oxygen that he kept in the plane for high altitude flying, then struggled through the snow, following the rope until the snow disappeared in front of him. Above him, he could hear the drone of Skip's engine as he circled, looking for his own spot to land. He tugged on the rope. "Hey, can you hear me?"

A weak shout came back at him. "Oh, God. I thought I heard a plane. I'm tangled in my ropes. You'll have to pull me out."

Joe sat in the snow and dug his heels into the icy surface, then grabbed the rope and began to haul the climber up over the edge. To his relief, she wasn't a large woman and she had enough strength to help him along.

Finally, her parka hood appeared in the snow in front of him.

By the time he reached her, she'd collapsed. Placing the mask over her frostbitten face, he ordered her to breathe. Then he pushed her goggles up on her forehead and watched as her eyes fluttered open. A weak smile curled the corners of her lips. "Are you real?" she croaked.

Joe gave the woman his most charming smile, but it was hidden behind the flap of his down jacket. Even her frostbitten cheeks and nose didn't obliterate her pretty face. "Yeah, I'm real. And you're lucky to be alive."

"I didn't think I'd ever get out of that crevasse," she murmured with her lilting accent. "I spent the night there just barely hanging on."

"Can you stand?"

She nodded and he helped her to her feet, holding the oxygen mask over her face. Wrapping her arm around his shoulders, he pulled her toward the plane.

"I owe you my life," she said, gasping for breath as she placed one foot in front of the other.

Joe smiled inwardly, his mind anticipating the reaction he'd get back at the lodge. Both Hawk and Tanner had marveled at his particular talent with women. To the amazement of both of his buddies, he always managed to find himself in the company of the most beautiful women Alaska had to offer. And now he'd done it again, finding a beautiful blonde in a crevasse on the Kahiltna Glacier.

"No problem," he said. "It's my mission in life to rescue damsels in distress."

She stopped to draw a few deep breaths then looked up at him. "I don't know how I can ever repay you."

Joe grinned. He was a lucky man, in more ways than

one. "How about dinner? I mean, after you've had a chance to thaw out. I know this nice little place in Talkeetna that serves great pasta."

PERRIE KINCAID PULLED the collar of her jacket up around her neck and cursed at the cold, unrelenting drizzle. Her eyes scanned the dark street from her spot in the shadow of a deserted building, then came back to the black Mercedes parked next to the loading dock. A bare lightbulb swung slowly in the salt-tanged breeze, sending an eerie wavering light over the battered steel door of the abandoned brick warehouse.

Inside the car, the glow of a cigarette illuminated the profile of the driver. Mad Dog Scanlon. She'd been following Mad Dog's boss so long, Perrie felt as if she and the goon were old friends. She squinted at her watch, then drew a deep breath and cursed again. "Come on, what's taking them so long? It's a simple deal, in and out. All I need is a good look at their faces, just confirmation, and then this story is front-page news."

The smell of salt water surrounded her, drifting inland from the sound with the constant damp that seemed to hang over the city of Seattle in the wintertime. She shifted on her feet and rubbed her hands together, trying to warm her icy fingers. If she had to wait much longer, she might just start to mildew, right along with everything else in this seedy neighborhood.

She should be used to the weather by now. Seattle had been her home ever since she'd left grad school ten years ago. She'd come west, from the University of Chicago, to take a job at the *Seattle Star*. At first she had written obituaries, then moved up to a job in the Lifestyles section. She'd almost been stuck writing fluff for the rest of her career, when the city desk put out a call for a staff writer.

Perrie had begged Milt Freeman, the city editor, to take her on, to give her a chance with hard news, even though she'd been writing gardening and cooking articles for the previous three years. After a week of constant appeals and a case of his favorite scotch, he had finally relented and offered her the job.

Milt had told her afterward that he'd been worn down by her tenacity—not the scotch—the same tenacity that she'd used to become the *Star*'s top investigative reporter. The same stubborn determination she was drawing on this very minute. A good reporter would long for a hot bath and a warm bed right about now. But Perrie considered herself a great reporter, and she was exactly where she wanted to be. Right in the thick of things.

Perrie Kincaid's byline was hot. She had broken four major stories in Seattle in the past two years, and three of them had been picked up by the national wire services. Her peers in the broadcast industry were in awe of her, unable to snatch even the smallest scoops from under her perceptive gaze. And drizzle or none, she was going to break this story, too.

The seemingly abandoned warehouse was actually the nerve center of a major smuggling ring that dealt in stolen luxury autos, cars that had probably been parked in front of one of Seattle's trendy restaurants just hours before. Once stolen, they were loaded into containers and shipped to the Far East, where they were traded for uncut heroin, which was then loaded on the boat for the return trip to Seattle.

The smuggling ring was only a small part of the story. There had been blackmail and attempted murder. But the part that would nab her the Pulitzer was the trail that led right to the floor of the U.S. Congress, to the dishonorable congressman from the great state of Washington, Evan T. Dearborn.

Somewhere inside the warehouse, Dearborn's chief of staff was meeting with Mad Dog's boss, the man in charge of this little operation, Seattle businessman and resident sleazeball, Tony Riordan. For ten years, Riordan had been living on the edge of the law, always involved in something illegal but careful enough not to get caught—and using the profits from his "business" dealings to buy a politician or two. He'd snagged a big one when he'd snagged Dearborn.

Well, Riordan was about to go down, and he was going to take a whole host of his slimy friends with him, including the congressman. The police had been on Riordan's tail for almost as long as Perrie had. Perrie reached into her pocket and fingered her cell phone. Sooner or later she'd have to call in the cops. But not until she had the final piece of the puzzle, hard evidence that would link the congressman's office to Tony Riordan. And not until her story was in black and white for all to see.

The sound of a car door opening brought her attention back to the Mercedes and she watched as Mad Dog stepped out of the car. With nervous hands, she reached for the camera that was slung over her shoulder, praying the shutter hadn't rusted tight in the two hours she'd been standing in the rain. She pulled off the lens cover, then held the camera up to her eye and focused the telephoto lens on the doorway.

A moment later two figures emerged, flanked by a pair of Tony's hulking bodyguards. Perrie smiled to herself as she recognized Tony and the congressman's chief of staff in the viewfinder. Calmly, she refocused and slid her finger to the shutter. But just as she was about to snap her first photo, the sound of a ringing cell phone fractured the quiet of the night.

Startled, Perrie looked over the top of the camera, wondering who would be calling Riordan at two in the morning. But as the phone rang again, she realized that the group on the loading dock was looking in *her* direction. The sound was coming from her coat pocket! In a flash, the two goons on the dock pulled guns and all hell broke loose.

Perrie dropped the camera and fumbled for her cell phone just as the first shot whizzed past her head and careened off the building behind her. She slid deeper into the shadows and flipped open the phone, wincing as another bullet hissed a little too close.

"Perrin? Perrin, is that you?"

Perrie groaned at the sound of her mother's voice. "Mom, I can't talk right now. I'll call you back." She ducked her head as another shot hit the brick wall above her.

"Perrie, this will just take a minute."

"Mom, it's two in the morning!"

"Honey, I know you don't sleep soundly and I figured you were up anyway. I just wanted to let you know that Mrs. Wilke's son is coming home for a visit. He's a dentist, you know, and a bachelor. I think it would be nice if—Perrin? Is that a gunshot I heard?"

Perrie cursed out loud, then slowly worked her way along the base of the wall. "Mother, I really can't talk now! I'll call you back in a few minutes." She flipped off the phone, then dialed 911, her fingers trembling.

When the operator answered, she quickly gave her name and her location. From where she sat, huddled in the dark, it sounded as if she were in the middle of a war zone. The gunfire was coming from two directions now, and she seemed to be caught right in the line of fire.

Were the cops already on the scene? Or was there another piece to this puzzle she didn't know about? She slid over and risked a look at the melee across the street. Riordan's men were still shooting at her, but someone else was shooting at them. Her missing puzzle piece was heavily armed with semiautomatic weapons, that much she could tell.

"Ma'am, please stay on the line. Is the shooting still going on?"

"Yes, it's still going on!" Perrie shouted. "Can't you hear it?" She held the phone out, giving the operator a taste of her predicament.

"Just remain calm, ma'am."

"I've got to get my camera," she said, realizing it was the first calm and rational thought she'd had since the shooting started.

"Ma'am, stay right where you are. We'll have a car there in about two minutes."

"I need my camera." Perrie slid along the base of the building, back the way she'd come, her eyes fixed on the camera lying near a puddle of water on the rain-slicked pavement. Stretching her arm out, she reached for the strap just inches away from her fingertips. Another gunshot whizzed by and she could almost feel its heat through her jacket sleeve. She winced, then made one desperate lunge for the camera strap.

Her fingers closed around it and she dragged it and herself back to the safety of the shadows. "A picture is worth a thousand words," she muttered as she wiped off the wet lens with her jacket cuff. "Not a thousand of *my* words. A picture would only be worth about a hundred of my words." Her gaze fixed on a dark patch on her sleeve and she sighed as she tried to brush the mud away.

But it wasn't mud on her sleeve. The touch of her own fingers sent a shard of pain up her arm and she blinked in surprise. "Oh, damn," she murmured, rubbing the sticky blood between her fingers. "I've been shot."

A smile curled the corners of her mouth and she giggled to herself, half out of shock and half out of disbelief. "I've been shot." She picked up the cell phone. "I've been shot," she repeated to the emergency operator.

"Ma'am, you say you've been shot?"

"I've always wondered what it would feel like," Perrie explained. "A bullet piercing your own skin. Would it feel hot or cold? Would you know it happened right away or would it take a while?" She closed her eyes and fought back a wave of lightheadedness.

"Ma'am, please don't move. We'll have a car there in thirty seconds. And an ambulance is on the way. Can you tell me where you've been shot? Please, ma'am, stay right where you are."

"I'm not going anywhere," Perrie said as she tipped her head back to rest on the rough brick wall. The rain spattered on her face and she welcomed the cold. It was the only thing that seemed real about this whole incident. "Wild horses couldn't drag me away from this story now," she murmured as the wail of sirens echoed in the distance.

The next half hour passed in a blur of flashing red lights and frantic paramedics. They had hustled her inside an ambulance and bandaged her arm, but she'd refused to be transported to the hospital, choosing instead to watch the scene unfold in the rainy night in front of the warehouse, questioning the detectives who collected the evidence of the shootout.

"Perrie!"

She glanced over her shoulder once to see Milt Freeman approaching, his expression filled with fury. Ignoring his summons, she turned back to the detective and continued her own interrogation.

"Damn it, Kincaid, what the hell happened here?"

"I'm sure you know all about it by now," Perrie called.

The detective looked up as Milt grabbed her arm. She winced in pain and Milt frowned. "Get her to the hospital," the detective advised. "And get her out of my hair. She took a bullet in the arm."

"What?" Milt boomed.

"I'm fine," Perrie insisted, her attention on the detective. "Why don't you let me get a peek at that wallet?"

The detective gave Milt an exasperated look, then walked away, shaking his head.

"This is it," Milt said, drawing her along toward the ambulance. "Two weeks ago, they tampered with the brakes on your car. Last week, they broke into your apartment. And now you're dodging bullets in the middle of a wise-guy war. I want you out of Seattle. Tonight."

"Yeah, right. Where am I going to go?" Perrie asked.

"Alaska," Milt said, pushing her down to sit on the wide bumper of the ambulance.

"Alaska?" Perrie gasped. "I'm not going to Alaska."

"You're going," Milt countered. "And I don't want you to give me any grief about it. You were shot tonight and you're acting like it was just another day at the office."

"It was only a flesh wound," she grumbled, glancing at the bandage around her arm. "The bullet just grazed me." She grinned at her boss. He was not nearly as amused as she was. "Milt, I can't believe I just said that. This is like those guys that used to cover combat zones in Vietnam. I feel like I've finally earned my stripes. I'm not some wimpy Lifestyles writer anymore. I've actually been wounded in the line of duty."

Milt crossed his arms over his chest and leaned back against the rear door of the ambulance, sending Perrie a disapproving glare. "I've called an old friend of mine up in a little town called Muleshoe. Joe Brennan is his name. He runs an air charter service. I go fishing up there in the summer and he always flies me in and out. He owes me a few favors."

Perrie ignored his story and concentrated on her own. Milt was a little upset right now. He'd get over it. "The way I see it, we should run the story now. As far as I'm concerned, we've got all the confirmation we need. So I didn't get a picture. I saw Dearborn's chief of staff there with Riordan. That's the connection."

Milt cursed softly. "All I see here is two dead wise guys and no sign of either Dearborn or Riordan. You've got a big empty hole where you thought you had a solid story."

"I do have a story!" Perrie protested. "And it's here, not in Alaska."

Milt Freeman leveled his gaze on hers. "You're acting like Alaska is Siberia. It *is* one of the fifty states, you know."

"Yeah, but it used to be Siberia," she shot back. "Before we bought it from the Russians. I'm so close on this story, Milt, I can smell the ink already. I just need a few more pieces of the puzzle and we can run with it."

"What you have right now, Perrin Kincaid, is a price on your head. Someone knows you're onto this story and they're not about to let you write it."

Perrie stood. "I've got to get back to the office."

"You're going to the hospital and then you're going to Alaska."

"My files are back at the office. I've got work to do."

"You can turn all your files over to me," Milt said. "And I'll give them to the police."

"You'll do no such thing!"

"And I sent Ginny over to your house to pack some clothes for you. After the doctors check you out, I'm taking you to the airport."

"I'm not going to Alaska," she repeated.

"Whoever shot you tonight will be looking for a second chance. And I've spent too much time turning you from a Lifestyles hack into a decent reporter to have you end up dead. You're going to Alaska, Kincaid."

She shook her head stubbornly. "No, I'm not. I'm staying right here and I'm going to break this story. Now, what do you think about—"

"The police are going to break this story," he interrupted. "After they figure out who shot you, you can come back and write it." He reached into his jacket pocket and held out an envelope. "I had a feeling something like this was going to happen. There's an airline ticket to Fairbanks in there. Joe Brennan will fly you into Muleshoe. I've got a nice safe, cozy cabin for you there. No phones, no bullets, no wise guys. Just peace and quiet. I even asked Joe to stock it with popcorn since you seem to think it's a fair substitute for all of the major food groups. I want you somewhere safe until things cool down around here."

She snatched her notepad from the back pocket of her jeans, wincing as a pain shot down to her fingers, then scribbled an errant thought about the evening's events. "I'm not going, Milt," she said, flipping through her notes. "I have work to do. I won't just sit around all day long waiting for you to call me back here. I can't."

"That's why I've got you a story to cover," he continued. "And this is not a request, Ace—this is an order from your boss."

Perrie glanced up at him and laughed harshly. Milt rarely pulled rank on her. They were more a team than boss and employee. "Oh, yeah, right. What kind of story? Underworld kingpins set up shop in Mulesfoot, Alaska? I don't think so."

"Just last week, three young women from Seattle left their homes and their jobs and traveled to Muleshoe to become mail-order brides. They answered an ad in our paper. I heard your old boss in Lifestyles talking about it. She was planning to send a reporter up to cover their story. I convinced her we should send you."

"What?" Indignant, Perrie jumped up and paced back and forth in front of her boss. "You're sending me back to Lifestyles? God, Milt, I hate writing that dreck." She cursed a blue streak, then shook her head stubbornly. "I'm not going. You can fire me if you want, but I'm staying here to write this story."

Milt leaned closer, fixing Perrie with an intractable gaze. "You're going to Muleshoe, Perrin Kincaid. You're going to rest and recover from your wound and I will call you when it's safe to come back. This story will still be here, I promise."

"I'm not going," Perrie repeated. "I'm not. And you can't make me."

JOE BRENNAN STOOD silently in the waiting area and watched as a line of travelers straggled through the jet-way and into the airport. He glanced again at the board, just to make sure he was in the right place, then held the sign up a little higher. He'd written the name Mr. Perry Kincaid on the back of a battered fuel bill that he had yet to pay, but so far, no one had claimed the name.

Maybe the guy had missed his plane. Or maybe Milt Freeman had decided that whatever trouble his reporter was in, it could be best handled in Seattle. All Joe knew was that he owed Milt a few favors and Milt had finally called one in. Though he couldn't show Perry Kincaid much fun in the dead of an Alaskan winter, Hawk might be able to take him ice fishing.

He scanned the waiting area again and his gaze stopped on a young woman who was in the midst of a heated argument with the desk attendant. She wore a short leather jacket and jeans that hugged her backside perfectly. Her auburn hair had been piled haphazardly on top of her head, twisted into an off-center knot that seemed in jeopardy of slipping over her left ear. A bright yellow pencil jutted out of the knot and he watched as she shoved a pen in next to it.

Joe had learned to appreciate a good-looking woman when he could—whether half-frozen on Denali or in the midst of an argument in the airport. Muleshoe—and most of Alaska's bush country—was populated mainly by men, men who fished and hunted and searched for gold, or men who provided goods and services to those trying to eke out a living in the Alaskan bush. Muleshoe was not the kind of town that women found attractive—unless, of course, they were looking to get married.

Just last week, he'd flown in three women who had answered an ad in the *Seattle Star*. A group of single men in Muleshoe had decided that they'd never get wives unless the women knew they were looking, so they pooled their money and bought the ad. Erv Saunders asked Joe if he wanted in. For forty dollars, Joe could buy a chance to read through the letters, study the photos and pick himself a potential bride.

But Joe had taken a pass. A woman—especially a desperate woman bent on marriage—would only complicate his life. Besides, in order to get married, a guy would have to fall in love, and Joe Brennan had never been in love in his life. For now, he was more than satisfied with an occasional affair, no strings attached.

He studied the woman at the desk, pushing his sunglasses down and the brim of his baseball cap up to get a better look. His mind slowly formed an image of her face. But then, before the picture had completely materialized, she spun around suddenly. The image evaporated, replaced by one more lovely than he'd even anticipated. He fought back a purely instinctive jolt of desire, an unbidden and electric attraction, then shoved his sunglasses back up on his nose. He forced his gaze to fix somewhere over her right shoulder.

Lord, she was pretty, he thought as he risked another glance. Her auburn hair framed delicate features—wide eyes, a perfect nose, a lush mouth. He found his eyes drawn back to stare, against his will, and to his surprise, he found her staring back.

She narrowed her eyes and a defiant expression settled on her features. Squaring her shoulders, she started across the distance that separated them. Joe glanced to either side to make sure he hadn't misunderstood the object of her attention. No, she was definitely headed in his direction.

She stopped in front of him, gave him the once-over, then sighed. "All right, here I am," she snapped. "Now what are you supposed to do with me?"

Joe blinked, then slowly lowered the sign he held. "I beg your pardon?"

"You're Brennan, right?" She shifted the bag on her shoulder, then thrust out her hand. He hesitantly took it, holding her slender fingers against his palm. Another jolt of electricity, this time skittering up his arm. "I'm Perrie Kincaid."

He frowned, then shook his head. "You're Perry Kincaid? You're a woman."

She arched an eyebrow and regarded him coolly. "You've definitely been living in Siberia too long."

"I was expecting a man. Perry is a man's name. Like Perry Como. And Milt lead me to believe—"

"It's *i-e*, not *y*," she countered. "And you're not exactly what I expected, either."

His mouth quirked in amusement. Gee, she was a snotty little thing, all full of spit and vinegar. "And what did you expect?"

"Well, being an open-minded feminist, I should have expected Josephine Brennan. But to tell the truth, I expected some potbellied guy with fishing lures stuck in his hat and a cigar butt clenched in his teeth."

"Sorry to disappoint you, Miss Kincaid."

"It's Perrie. Or Kincaid. You can drop the Miss. Makes me sound like a damn debutante." Perrie shook her head and began to pace in front of him. "You know, I should have suspected he'd try something like this. First he confiscates my cell phone. Then he steals my wallet. I don't have a credit card to my name, all my cash is gone. I should have known there was something fishy when he offered to watch my stuff while I went to get a cup of coffee. Then he wouldn't leave the damn airport until my plane left the ground. I tried to get off twice and he was standing there blocking the door of the jetway. Then he tricks you into flying me into some frozen tundra town…Donkeyfoot or Mulefoot or whatever it's called." She smiled and patted the side of her shoulder bag. "But I got him back because I took all my files with me. He's got the key to my desk, but I took the evidence. He's got nothing to give the cops." She stopped, met his gaze and drew a deep breath. "So, what's it going to take, Brennan?"

She talked faster than anyone he'd ever met and it took him a moment to realize that she'd finished. "Take? I don't understand."

She rolled her eyes in exasperation. "Everyone has a price. What's yours? I'll pay you to fly me back to Seattle. Whatever your regular price is, I'll double it. I can't pay you up front, but as soon as we get back I'll pay you in cash. I've got important business back there and I can't waste another minute in igloo country."

Milt had warned him that Perrie Kincaid would try to talk him into taking him back…or her. Damn, this was all he needed! Milt knew exactly how he'd react to the prospect of baby-sitting some hyperactive, run-at-the-mouth woman reporter, especially one with such an attitude. He would have refused, flatly and quickly. But now that she was here, he was stuck with her.

"Do you have luggage?" he asked.

She took his question for acquiescence and smiled in satisfaction. "It will only take a minute for me to pick it up. So, how long will it take to get back to Seattle?"

"Depends on the weather," he replied as he reached for her shoulder bag.

She pulled away from him. "I can carry my own bag, Brennan."

"Suit yourself...Kincaid."

"So...what? Four, five hours?"

"I said, it depends on the weather. There's weather coming in and we're going to have to move if we expect to beat it."

She automatically picked up her pace but he barely had to lengthen his stride to keep up. As they hurried down the concourse, he gave her a sideways glance. For all her beauty, Perrie Kincaid was the most prickly woman he'd ever met.

"I hope you brought something warmer to wear," he commented.

"Why?"

He shrugged. "It can get a little cold in my plane."

"Where is this plane of yours?"

"It's parked at a hangar on the other side of the airport. I've got a truck and we'll drive over as soon as we have your bag. Hopefully we'll get clearance to take off."

"Do we have to ask for clearance, Brennan? Why can't we just go?"

"If the tower advises me to stay on the ground, I stay on the ground. I don't know about you, Kincaid, but I happen to value my life—and my plane."

"Just because I managed to get myself shot does not mean I have a death wish, Brennan. Jeez, Milt is such a worrywart. What else did he tell you? Did he tell you that I was supposed to rest all day and take it easy? Three minutes in some backwoods cabin and I'll be crawling the walls."

Joe stared down at her as they walked, more baffled by this woman with every step. "Milt didn't tell me you'd been shot."

An impatient scowl marred her pretty features. "It was just a small flesh wound. It hardly hurts at all. But Milt seems to think if I stay in Seattle, something more serious is going to happen."

"Milt is probably right."

She stopped cold and groaned, throwing down her bag and planting her hands on her slender waist. "Don't you start on me now, Brennan. I am perfectly capable of taking care of myself. I don't need Milt or you or anyone else telling me how to live my life."

Cursing beneath his breath, Joe grabbed her arm with one hand and her bag with the other and dragged her along with him. "I was simply stating an opinion, Kincaid." She didn't seem like a "Miss" Kincaid to him anymore. And calling her Perrie felt entirely too personal.

"I'm not interested in your opinions," she muttered. "I just want to get home."

She picked up her pace, yanking her arm from his grasp. He took a moment to admire her backside again, the cute wiggle of her hips as she strode down the concourse. He grinned when she stopped and looked back at him impatiently.

"What's the problem?"

He caught up to her. "I don't know why you're so anxious to get home. Milt says you're in danger."

"My boss can be a bit melodramatic."

"Hey, I've got a lot of respect for Milt Freeman. He's a good guy. You should be happy someone like him is looking out for you."

She didn't have a comeback for that. Instead, she sent him an obstinate glare and refused to say another word until they'd recovered her bag and headed for the doors. When they stepped outside, a wickedly cold wind slapped them both in the face and snow swirled around their feet.

"Jeez," she hissed, her teeth chattering. "Is it always so blasted cold here?"

Joe glanced up at the late afternoon sky. The weather was moving in faster than he'd expected. If they didn't get off the ground quickly, he'd be spending the rest of the day and probably a major portion of his evening with Perrie Kincaid. His jaw tightened. To hell with the tower. He'd go whether they gave him the okay or not. "You're in Alaska, Kincaid. What did you expect, palm trees and ocean breezes?"

She gave him that look again, the one that told him she was about to start another harangue. "I expected—"

"The truck's in the lot," Joe said, interrupting her before she had another chance to start talking. He grabbed her arm again and pulled her along. Damn if he wasn't beginning to like Perrie Kincaid better when she had her mouth shut.

They made it to the hangar without further argument, Perrie choosing to sit silently beside him, her eyes fixed on the road. To Joe's relief, the plane was fueled and ready to go when he pulled up. He parked the truck, then ran around the front to open Perrie's door, but she'd already jumped out and was dragging her bag from the back on her own.

Satisfied that she could take care of herself, he tugged his hat down and ran over to Tanner O'Neill, who was standing by the hangar door. "What's the weather look like?" Joe asked. "Are they going to let us go?"

Tanner shouted against the frigid Arctic wind. "If you get off the ground in the next fifteen minutes, you should be all right. You'll be ahead of the storm all the way to Muleshoe. I put the mail sack in back and there's a crate of fresh mushrooms that Burdy ordered for the spaghetti feed at the fire hall Saturday night. There's a load of lumber in the cabin, I've tied it all down. Tell Hawk to unload it and put it in the shed for now."

Joe nodded. He hadn't seen Tanner in more than a week. He and Julia had been married in Muleshoe the weekend before last and had decided on a family honeymoon at Disney World with Julia's nine-year-old son, Sammy. They'd returned and decided to stay in Fairbanks and look for an apartment, where they'd live during the winter months while Sam was in school.

"How is Sam?" Joe asked.

"Sammy loved Florida but misses you and Hawk and the lodge. And Julia is in the middle of tying up all her business affairs in Chicago. By the way, we've made a decision."

"What's that?"

"We're not going to live in Fairbanks during the winter. We've decided to live at the lodge. Sammy will go to school in Muleshoe."

Joe grinned, happy that he'd have his partner at the lodge full-time, not to mention Sammy and his mom. He'd grown to love the kid and appreciate his mother. Julia made Tanner happier than a man had any right to be. Someday, when Joe was ready to settle down, he hoped to find a woman as sweet and loving as Julia Logan.

But for now, he was left with Perrie Kincaid—a first-rate pain in the backside. She joined them, standing beside Joe, her hair now free of its knot and whipping in her face. "Are we going to be able to get to Seattle?"

Tanner frowned, then opened his mouth, but Joe shot him a warning glare. "Tanner O'Neill, meet Perrie Kincaid," Joe said. "Go stow your luggage in the plane, Kincaid, and hop in. I'll be there in a second."

They both watched her hurry toward the Otter, then Tanner grabbed Joe's arm and pointed at her. "How the hell do you do it, Brennan? You were supposed to pick up some guy from the airport and you end up with a woman. And a beautiful woman to boot."

Joe grinned. "Pure, unadulterated charm."

"If you take her to Seattle, you're going to be flying right into that storm."

Joe chuckled and patted his buddy on the shoulder. "Don't worry. We're not going to Seattle. She just thinks we are. We're on our way to Muleshoe like I promised her boss."

"You're going to put her up at the lodge?" Tanner asked. "Are you sure you want to test the legend again? I let Julia in the door and I ended up marrying her."

Joe shook his head. When Julia Logan had showed up at Bachelor Creek Lodge, Joe had been the first one to move out. Legend claimed that a woman entering Bachelor Creek Lodge was destined to marry one of the occupants and Joe wasn't about to take any chances. The legend had proved true, but Tanner had been the one to be caught. "Perrie Kincaid is staying in one of the guest cabins."

Tanner blinked. "She isn't going to be so happy with that. No indoor plumbing. In the middle of winter."

"Well, she'll have to live with it," Joe replied. "She's not setting foot in the lodge."

Tanner glanced over at Perrie, then back at Joe. "She doesn't look like the type to live with anything she doesn't like."

"I know," Joe grumbled. "But I'll deal with that problem later."

PERRIE HUDDLED DOWN in the copilot's seat, wrapping her arms around herself and stamping her feet. Her breath clouded in front of her and her nose was so cold she was sure it would break off if she rubbed it. "Don't you have any heat in this plane?"

Brennan glanced at her absently, as if surprised that he had a passenger at all. He hadn't said a word since they'd taken off an hour before and seemed quite comfortable with the silence. He closed his hand into a fist and rapped firmly on a spot near the center of the control console. A fan began to whir and, slowly, the cockpit of the Otter warmed to a temperature somewhere above freezing.

"I sure hope the rest of your plane works better than the heater," she muttered.

He grunted in reply, his expression hidden behind his sunglasses and shadowed by the brim of his cap. He seemed intent on the view through the plane's windshield, so Perrie took the opportunity to study him.

She considered herself an excellent judge of character, possessed of the ability to immediately discern a person's true nature and hidden agendas with a simple glance. It had come in handy in her work, allowing her to cut through the bull and get right to the heart of the matter. But Joe Brennan defied an immediate impression.

His physical attributes were simple enough. A long, lean body. Thick, dark hair badly in need of a trim. A handsome face behind the shadowy stubble of a three-day beard. But she'd have to see his eyes to really get a good take on him. And since they'd met, he'd kept his eyes hidden behind his sunglasses.

Perrie turned her gaze to the landscape below them, searching for the first sight of civilization. But all she saw was forest, broken only by spots and strings of white that she guessed were lakes and rivers in the summer. When she couldn't discern their location, she turned her attention back to the pilot.

Why bother to figure out Joe Brennan? It was a waste of energy. After they landed in Seattle and she paid him off, she'd never see him again. What did she care what kind of character lurked behind his shades? As long as he was a capable pilot, she didn't need to know more.

"How much longer until we land in Seattle?" she asked. "I would have thought we could see the coastline by now. Are we going to have enough gas? Or will we have to stop? I could really go for a cup of coffee right about now."

"There's a thermos behind my seat," he said. "And we're not going to Seattle."

Perrie chuckled and peered out the window. "Of course we're—" Her words died in her throat and she slowly turned to him. "What do you mean, we're not going to Seattle? I'm paying you to take me there."

"I'm taking you to Muleshoe, just like I promised Milt Freeman."

She twisted in her seat, snatching at her seat belt with

frantic fingers. "We had a deal, Brennan. Turn this plane around and take me to Seattle."

He turned to her and pushed his sunglasses down on his nose. Brilliant blue eyes sparkled with amusement—and challenge. He met her gaze without blinking and she felt a slow shiver work its way down her spine. For a moment, she couldn't breathe for staring at him.

He made a lazy survey of her face and then her body, and she wondered how many times she'd been observed in the same way from behind the reflective lenses. But her instincts suddenly failed her, for all she could read in Joe Brennan's blue eyes was an instant and undisguised sexual curiosity. A curiosity she shared at that very moment.

The realization rocked her senses and an unexpected flood of desire warmed her blood. She forced herself to glance away, certain that his gorgeous eyes were somehow to blame for her momentary lapse. The guy was a first-class charmer, all right, and he was using his charm to renegotiate the terms of their agreement, employing every available weapon, including her newfound weakness for a handsome face and devilish grin. Well, she wasn't going to fall for it. "I—I want to go back to Seattle," she said, trying to cover a tremor in her voice.

His eyebrow quirked up. "You seem to forget who's flying this plane, Kincaid. You go where I go. Unless, of course, you want to jump. I don't have a parachute with me, but that shouldn't matter to a woman like you."

Azure. His eyes were really more azure than sapphire. The same clear blue of the sky outside. She swallowed hard and ignored the heat that rose from her throat to her face. "What is that supposed to mean? A woman like me."

"I know your type. Nothing stands in your way, does it?"

No, Perrie never let anything stand between her and her work. But somehow, coming from him, the comment felt more like an insult. She bristled, her sudden attraction now tempered with defiance. "The hell if I'm going to Donkeyleg," she shot back. With a curse, she grabbed the controls on her side of the plane.

He chuckled, then leaned back in his seat, crossing his arms over his chest and watching her expectantly. "You want to fly her, be my guest. If you can get us back to Seattle, the ride's on me, sweetheart."

She'd never driven a plane before, but it couldn't be all that complicated. She was an intelligent woman, a woman who had once driven in downtown Chicago during a rush-hour snowstorm. At least up here there were no speeding taxis and bothersome pedestrians. There was only up and down and left and right. Though down wasn't a direction she really wanted to explore right at this moment.

Placing her feet on the pedals, she gripped the steering yoke with white-knuckled hands. "You think I can't fly this plane, don't you?" Her words came out through clenched teeth.

"I *know* you can't fly this plane. But I'm willing to give you a chance."

Grinding her teeth, she slowly turned the steering yoke. The plane responded by making a gentle bank to the right. But as she turned, the plane's nose tipped down slightly. Her eyes went wide.

"You're losing altitude," he commented.

"I know that." She closed her eyes and tried to remember everything she knew about airplanes, then slowly pulled back on the yoke. The plane's nose began to rise again and a self-satisfied smile curled her lips. This wasn't so tough. She glanced at the compass. South. They'd have to head south to get to Seattle. And when they got there, she'd make a try at landing the plane. If she knew one thing about Joe Brennan, he wouldn't let her crash his precious plane over the stupid game they were playing.

"Before you fly into that weather ahead, you better file a new flight plan with Fairbanks. They'll need to know what part of the wilderness to search after we go down."

"We're not going down," she said.

"If you fly us into that storm, Kincaid, I can guarantee we'll go down. The wings will ice up and we won't have enough power to maintain our air speed. We'll slowly lose altitude and we'll probably crash somewhere in the Alaska Range. Maybe if we're lucky, you'll hit Mount McKinley."

"You're enjoying this, aren't you?" she snapped.

"Immensely."

Perrie Kincaid did not accept defeat lightly. The truth be told, she couldn't remember the last time she'd thrown in the towel...except for the Saturday she had tried to fix the toilet in her apartment and it flooded the bathroom and the apartment below. A plumber had been her last resort, and she'd called one only after she'd exhausted all her other alternatives.

The dark clouds looming in front of them would more than likely put an end to her short career as a pilot. If she continued this game of one-upmanship with Joe Brennan, it might even end her life. Hell, she'd go to Donkeyleg with him. But she wouldn't let him win. She'd hop the first bus out of that freeze-dried burg and make her own way back to Seattle.

"All right, we'll do it your way," she said, taking her

hands off the controls. "For now," she added beneath her breath.

He grinned, shoved his sunglasses back up, then slowly banked the plane until they were headed northeast again. "I think you'll find Muleshoe infinitely more bearable than crashing into a snow-covered mountainside. We've got a tavern, a general store, a mercantile and our own post office. And there's a spaghetti feed at the fire hall on Saturday night."

"Oh boy," Perrie muttered. "A spaghetti feed. I'll try to contain my excitement."

"WELCOME TO MULESHOE, Kincaid."

Joe watched Perrie peer through the frosty windshield of his Blazer, which he had parked in the middle of Main Street. She didn't have to look hard to see the town, mostly because the greater part of it lined one street.

The buildings were a ramshackle lot of faded paint and rickety porches, frosted windows and wisps of smoke curling around the chimney pipes. Front yards were cluttered with a variety of snow-covered possessions—old tires, dogsleds, snowshoes, fuel drums, rusted canoes, animal pelts—and anything else worth saving for future use. To the outsider, it might appear a bit shabby, but to Joe, it was home.

"Good grief," she muttered. "It's worse than I imagined."

Joe bit back a snide retort. Right now, he wasn't in the mood to get into another "discussion" with Perrie Kincaid, especially in defense of the place he chose to live. "The lodge is about a mile north of town."

"And where do you live?"

"I live at the lodge," he replied.

Perrie gasped. "I'm staying with you?"

"Actually, you're staying in one of our guest cabins on the property. It's a real nice little place. You'll be warm and cozy. I had Burdy McCormack supply the place with everything you'll need for your stay. If I know Burdy, he's got a fire blazing in the stove and a pot of coffee brewing. He'll be your neighbor. After the Yukon freezes, he comes in from his claim and spends the winter in the cabin next to yours. Burdy makes a run into Muleshoe every day, so if you need something from town or you need a ride in, just flip up the flag on your front porch and he'll stop."

She slowly released a long breath and rubbed her arms. "Don't bother with the cabin, Brennan. Just take me to the nearest public transportation. The bus station will do."

When was she going to give up? He swore he'd never met a more pigheaded, single-minded woman in his life. And why he found her attractive, he'd yet to figure out. "I can't do that," he replied, leaning back in his seat and fixing her with a weary look.

"You might as well." She tipped her chin up in a way that had already become familiar to him. "I'll just walk there on my own. You can't stop me from leaving."

"That would be a little tough, seeing as the nearest bus station is halfway back to Fairbanks."

Perrie closed her eyes, her jaw tightening. *Here it comes*, he thought to himself. She'd been itching for another go-round since their confrontation in the plane and he knew he was about to feel the sting of her tongue. But she slowly schooled her temper and forced a smile. "All right, I'll just stand here on Main Street and stick out my thumb. There's bound to be a truck that comes by headed for civilization. Unless you're going to tell me you don't have roads and trucks up here."

"Oh, we have roads. Trucks, too. But not in the winter. This is the end of the highway, Kincaid, and once you're in Muleshoe after the first big snow, you're pretty much here for the duration. Until the spring thaw, that is."

Perrie arched her eyebrow dubiously. "What about this road? Where does it go?"

"Right now, not much of anywhere. Erv runs the plow. He keeps the road clear out to the airstrip and north to just beyond the lodge. But trying to clear the snow any further is like dusting in a sandstorm. Once you're finished, a new storm just moves in and blocks the roads again."

"Do you mean to tell me that there's no way out of town?"

"Sure there is. In my plane. But you already know I'm not real partial to that idea."

Narrowing her eyes, Perrie cursed beneath her breath. Then she grabbed the door handle and jumped out of the truck. As soon as she hit the ground, her feet slipped out from under her on the hard-packed snow. She steadied herself against the truck then began to pace. "What about food?" she said, stopping to stick her head through the open truck door.

"We bring that in by truck in the fall. Mostly canned and dried. We've got fresh meat frozen over at Kelly's meat locker. Venison, moose, caribou, salmon and a few sides of beef, as well. But if you're looking for fresh fruits and vegetables, you're pretty much out of luck. I bring in what I can, but only when I've got room in the plane."

She paced back and forth a few more times, nervous energy vibrating from her body with each step, then stopped again. "What happens when someone gets sick?"

"If it's an emergency, I fly them out. Or they send up

an evac plane from the hospital in Fairbanks. And if the weather is bad, well, then your chances aren't the best. This is a hard life up here, Kincaid. You're pretty much standing on the edge of the frontier. Once you cross the Yukon River, there's not another town for at least two hundred miles."

She clenched her fists and snarled in frustration. Hell, she even looked beautiful when she was angry and about to spit nails. Color rose in her cheeks and her green eyes came alive with light, and he found himself unable to keep from staring.

"How do people get to work?" she snapped.

"Everyone works on the land. They hunt and fish. They get by."

She stopped her pacing in front of him and scrambled back into the truck. Desperation filled her gaze and she reached out and grabbed the lapels of his jacket, then yanked him close. "I have got to get out of here, Brennan. You can take me right now, or I'll start walking. Either way, I'm going back to Seattle."

He pulled off his sunglasses and leaned closer, his mouth hovering over hers, his jaw tight with anger. He could feel her warm breath as it clouded up around his face in the cold. A tiny thread of desire snaked through him and his gaze skipped to her lips. An unbidden urge to cover her mouth with his own teased at his mind. Would her lips be as soft as they looked? How would she taste? And would a kiss finally shut her up?

He gripped the steering wheel with one hand until his fingers went numb. He didn't want to kiss her. What he really wanted to do was shake her until her teeth rattled. "Damn it, Kincaid, don't be a fool. If you try to walk out of here, you'll be dead in a day. The weather can change in the blink of an eye. There's a reason the road is closed.

So fools like you won't risk their necks trying to travel. You're here until I fly you out, and the sooner you get that through your stubborn head, the better."

She blinked, then frowned, drawing back slightly to look at him. Her gaze flitted over his angry expression, her eyes wide. Finally, he thought to himself, realization. After all this wasted time bickering with her, she'd decided to listen to reason. Maybe now she'd quit fighting the inevitable. She was here to stay until Milt Freeman told him it was safe to fly her out again.

"You want to kiss me, don't you?" Her husky voice was mixed with an equal measure of surprise and smug satisfaction.

A sharp laugh burst from his throat, but it sounded hollow and forced. He shifted in his seat, but she wouldn't let go of his jacket. What the hell? Was she a mind reader as well as a major pain in the backside? Or was his desire so easy to discern?

It had been a while since he'd had a woman. In fact, he'd been afraid to admit that he was going through a bit of a slump lately. There had been plenty of possibilities, plenty of romantic dinners, but that was about it. Not prepared to risk betraying another errant impulse to her prying gaze, he turned and looked out the front windshield, slowly slipping his sunglasses back on. "You have a rather high opinion of yourself, don't you, Kincaid?"

She sighed, then released his lapels and pushed away from him impatiently. "It's no big deal. I mean, why try to hide it? You're a healthy guy, living up here in the middle of nowhere. I'm an attractive, educated woman. You can say it, Brennan. I'm certainly not a prude. I'll admit it—I find myself slightly attracted to you, as well. Inexplicable, but an attraction nonetheless."

He reached for the key and started the truck, taking a small measure of satisfaction that the attraction was reciprocated. Still, all his good sense told him that pursuing Perrie Kincaid would be a colossal mistake. The sooner he dumped her at her cabin, the sooner he'd be able to escape from those disturbing green eyes. She was far too perceptive—and outspoken—for his tastes. Even if she was the only decent-looking woman in a fifty-mile radius. "Are you always so blunt?"

"I don't consider it a failing," she said. "In my line of work, it's a necessity. I always say what's on my mind. Why waste time dancing around the issue when you can cut right to the chase? It saves a lot of time and trouble."

"Well, as long as you're here in Muleshoe, you may want to tone it down a bit. You'll make more friends if you don't go blurting out every thought that comes into your head. Especially your rather negative opinions about Muleshoe."

"I'm not planning to stick around long enough to make friends."

"Whatever you say, Kincaid," he muttered, shifting the truck into drive and punching the accelerator. The back end fishtailed until he brought it under control. "I just don't want to be putting you in Kelly's meat locker."

"You'd lock me in a meat locker to keep me here?"

"No, that's where we put our dead folks until we can fly them out to the funeral home in Fairbanks. If you're planning to try to get out on your own, you'll end up there sooner or later."

She wriggled down in her seat and shot him an uneasy look. "I'll keep that in mind, Brennan."

As they drove down Main Street, Joe pointed out the major landmarks—the general store, the tavern, the mercantile, the post office—but she showed little interest. "And that's the brides' house, right over there." He pointed to a little cabin with smoke curling out of the stone chimney. "The bachelors built it last summer when they cooked up their mail-order plan. They figured to bring the brides up in the middle of the winter to test their mettle. If they could survive the snow and cold, then they might just be worth marrying. You might want to stop by and say hello. The three of them are the greatest concentration of the female sex you're likely to see between here and Fairbanks."

"I don't think we'll have a lot in common," she said, giving the cabin no more than a cursory glance.

"You never know."

"I'm supposed to write an article about them. Milt assigned it to me before he banished me from Seattle. I can't imagine why any woman in her right mind would choose to live out here."

"It's not all that bad," he said, wondering why he even bothered to defend it to her. "Some women find it a challenge. Not everyone loves living shoulder to shoulder in a city. All the noise, the pollution...the crime. I wouldn't be surprised if you got to like it a little bit."

"I wouldn't hold my breath if I were you." She leaned her head against the window and observed the scenery in silence.

Joe carefully negotiated the curve out of town, swinging his truck wide around a snowdrift that the wind had kicked up. He sure hoped Milt Freeman knew what he was doing sending Perrie Kincaid to Muleshoe. More than a few women and a good number of men had cracked under the endless boredom and isolation of an Alaskan winter. If the snow and cold didn't get to a person, the endless nights would. Days were short and darkness came early.

He didn't want to be around when Perrie Kincaid started suffering the combined effects of cabin fever and sunshine deprivation. The sooner Milt Freeman and the Seattle police solved her problems, the better off he'd be.

The better off they'd all be.

3

PERRIE LEANED BACK against the rough plank door and listened as Joe Brennan's footsteps crunched in the snow on the way back to his cabin. She was grateful to finally be out of range of those disturbing blue eyes of his. With a groan she let her shoulder bag slip to the floor. A few seconds later, she followed it, sliding her back against the door until she sat down with a thump. "I'm in prison," she murmured as she rubbed her sore arm. "That's what this is. Nothing but a gulag with a lovely dead-animal decor." She sighed. "And a warden cute enough to curl a girl's toes."

She glanced around the cabin at the mounted antlers scattered about the room, then silently cursed Milt Freeman and the scumbag that shot her. If it hadn't been for that one stray bullet, Milt never would have sent her to Siberia. She'd still be in Seattle, working on her story, following leads, tracking down witnesses. Instead, the only thing she had to occupy her mind was a thwarted plan to escape Muleshoe...and the possibility that Joe Brennan might kiss her.

If she had the time to spend, she might find Joe Brennan more than a little intriguing. Perhaps they might enjoy a tumble or two before she headed out of town. After all, Perrie wasn't immune to the charms of a ruggedly handsome man. She'd had a few men in her life—purely on her own terms, of course. But none of them had lasted very long once they'd realized they didn't rank high on her list of priorities.

Besides, she had already counted at least five good reasons why Joe Brennan got under her skin, five good reasons why she couldn't even consider allowing him to kiss her—or tumble her into bed. And the biggest was his refusal to return her to Seattle. How could she possibly respect a man who had no respect at all for the importance of her work?

She scrubbed at her face with her hands. Right now, she didn't want to think about Brennan. Her misguided attraction to him would only serve to distract her from her cause—getting back to Seattle. And he had vowed no assistance on that front. "I'll find another way," she said. "There's got to be another way."

She clambered to her feet and took a slow tour around the cabin, dropping her jacket on the floor along the way. It was nice enough, kind of warm and cozy. The rough plank floors were covered with a colorful assortment of braided rag rugs, making the one large room seem as if it were actually three rooms. A fieldstone fireplace dominated the far wall; an overstuffed sofa and an antique rocker were arranged around it.

At the other end of the cabin, a pair of old iron beds and a scarred dresser served as the sleeping area. The beds were covered by pretty quilts and fluffy pillows. In the corner, a potbellied stove radiated a gentle warmth. Perrie held out her hands for a moment to warm them, then turned to survey the kitchen.

Like the rest of the cabin, it was simple. An electric hot plate, a small refrigerator and knotty pine cabinets that looked as if they'd been homemade. A vase of dried flowers sat in the center of the old oak table. She sighed and rubbed her hands together, then crossed the room to brush aside the drapes of one of the cabin's three windows.

She expected to take a look at the weather. But instead, a face, lined with age and grinning a toothless smile, stared back at her through the glass. She screamed and jumped away, her heart leaping into her throat. The man waved at her, then tapped on the glass and pointed to the door. He wore a fur hat with earflaps flopping at the sides, bouncing up and down until it looked as if he might just take off like some human gooney bird.

Who was this? Surely Muleshoe didn't boast its own Peeping Tom along with all its other civilized features, did it? Placing her hand to her chest, she waited until her pulse slowed, then walked over to the door and opened it a crack.

The face pressed up to the opening, still grinning. "Hey there! You must be the little lady from Seattle."

"I am," she said, wary. "Who are you? And why were you looking in my window?"

"Burdy McCormack's my name." He shoved his hand through the door and she reluctantly shook it before she pulled the door open. Burdy scampered inside with a bandy-legged gait. "Just thought I'd look in on you. Wasn't sure you were here yet."

A cold wind trailed after him and Perrie quickly swung the door shut. His grin faded and he scratched his whiskered chin. "Guess yer not too fond of dogs. Strike is housebroke."

She glanced between him and the door. "I'm sorry, is your dog outside?" She opened the door again and peered out, seeing nothing but snow and trees and a single track of footprints on the front steps. "I'm afraid he's not out here."

"Come on, Strike," Burdy called, waving his arm.

"Come on in out of the cold, you sorry mutt. That's a boy. Good dog."

Perrie watched as Burdy McCormack reached down and patted the space near his knee. Space that was not occupied by man nor beast—nor anything real, for that matter. She bit her bottom lip. Good grief, the poor old guy thought he had a dog with him!

For a moment, she considered leaving the door open in case she'd have to make a quick escape. But the cabin was growing colder by the second so she decided the risk was worth staying warm. "That's a nice dog you have. Obedient." She leaned back against the closed door.

Burdy nodded, his grin growing so wide it seemed to envelop his entire weatherworn face. "Took me a long time to train 'im. There weren't no dog along the whole Yukon that could hunt better. But we've both been gettin' old, so we spend most of our time sittin' next to a warm fire." He looked around the cabin. "So, you have everything you need here? Joe asked me to look in on you every now and then."

Perrie rubbed her palms together and studied Burdy McCormack shrewdly. He seemed harmless enough, the type that might be swayed to her cause. A man who showed concern over the comfort of his imaginary dog couldn't be as coldhearted as Joe Brennan had been. "Actually, there is one thing you could help me with. I can't seem to find the bathroom."

Burdy scratched his chin. "That's out back of the cabin in the little house with the moon on the door."

Perrie gasped. "An outhouse? In the middle of winter?" She turned and began to pace the room. "You've got to help me find a way out of here. I can live without television, I can live without junk food, but I cannot live without indoor plumbing. I won't!"

Burdy wagged a gnarled finger at her and shook his head. "Aw, no you don't! Joe warned me about you. Said you'd try to talk me into taking you outta here. That's not gonna happen. I ain't gonna fall for no sweet talk from a pretty lady."

She added another to her list of reasons why kissing Joe Brennan was out of the question. He had a big mouth. Jeez, the whole territory probably knew by now that she'd set herself on escaping Muleshoe. "You don't understand," Perrie said calmly. "I have to get back to Seattle. It's a matter of—of life or death. There's got to be a way out of here."

"There's plenty of ways outta town. More than seven or eight pilots living here, an' each with a nice little bush plane, too."

"Pilots? You mean Brennan doesn't own a monopoly on air travel?"

"Ma'am, this here's Alaska. Cain't git around without a plane."

"Then you have to take me to one of these pilots. I'd be willing to pay you. A lot. You could buy yourself anything. A—a new dog."

The old man chuckled. "Now, why would I want a new dog when I have Strike here? We get along real well and he's hardly no bother. Never barks and don't eat much, either."

"I can see that. He's just about faded away to nothing."

The meaning of her comment didn't seem to register with Burdy. Either the man was totally daft or...or he was totally daft. There was no other way about it. Joe

Brennan had left her in the care of a crazy man and his invisible dog.

Burdy shoved his hat back and stared at her with sparkling blue eyes. "Joe wouldn't like it much if I was to help you leave. And I 'spect he's let all the other pilots know that they won't be takin' you out, either. But I s'pose that ain't gonna stop you from tryin'."

"Not a chance," Perrie said. "There's got to be one pilot in this town willing to fly for cash."

Burdy sighed and rubbed his forehead. "Would you like to take a trip into Muleshoe? I was about to get me some dinner down at St. Paddy's and I'd sure love the comp'ny of a pretty girl like yourself."

"You have a church here?"

Burdy chuckled. "St. Paddy's ain't a church. It's the local tavern. It's run by Paddy Doyle. We took to calling it St. Paddy's since most of us spend our Sunday mornings there. He makes a mean Irish breakfast—fried eggs and potato cakes and soda farl and homemade sausage—but he don't allow talking during his church service."

"He's a priest, then?" she asked. A man of the cloth would have to help her. He'd see that she was being held against her will and would prevail upon a local pilot to fly her out.

"Well, he does preside over the town's funerals, but he ain't a priest proper. He just makes us watch church on his big-screen satellite TV."

Perrie's hopes faltered. No priest.

"We all put up with it since the breakfast is so good," Burdy continued, "and 'cause Paddy takes his religion serious. Mass starts at eight and breakfast is served right after."

Perrie found her mouth watering at Burdy's description of breakfast. She hadn't had anything to eat since the previous night. She refused to count airline food as food. And the cup of coffee she'd guzzled at the airport hadn't done much to diminish her hunger. Dinnertime was fast approaching, and with it the need to cook, a skill she'd never quite mastered beyond microwave popcorn.

"Do they serve a good evening meal down at St. Paddy's?"

"Best in town," Burdy replied. "Except for the Saturday feeds down at the fire hall. I do the cookin' then. Spaghetti feed tomorrow night."

"And do the town's pilots eat at Doyle's?"

"Most of 'em."

"Then I think I'll take that ride into town, Burdy. I'm feeling a little hungry and I'm not really up to cooking tonight."

Burdy nodded, his earflaps bouncing. "All right, then. You'll find yourself a warm jacket and some boots in the closet over there. I won't be takin' you out in the cold unless you're properly dressed for it when there's weather rollin' in. And if old Sarah gets it in her head she don't want to go into town, we'll end up walkin'."

"Is Sarah your wife?"

"Nah, she's the lodge's pickup truck. We get on pretty well most times, but she can be an ornery old thing. If she sees you comin' she might get a little jealous and decide she ain't gonna take us into Muleshoe."

Perrie looked up from the floor as she pulled on a pair of oversize rubber boots and shrugged into a down parka. An invisible dog, a jealous truck and an old man more than a few sandwiches shy of a picnic.

Just what else would Muleshoe have to offer in the way of entertainment?

DOYLE'S TAP TAVERN, or St. Paddy's as the locals called it, was already bustling with people when Burdy showed her inside. As she scanned the room, Perrie slowly realized that she was the only woman in the place. It didn't take long for the rest of Paddy's patrons to realize the same thing. Conversation slowly ground to a halt as every eye turned toward her.

Perrie forced a smile and reached for Burdy's arm. "Why are they all looking at me like that?" she murmured.

Burdy straightened and puffed out his chest. "I s'pose they're all wondering how an old coot like me managed to put such a fine-lookin' woman on my arm." He cleared his throat. "This here's Miz Perrie Kincaid. She'll be stayin' here in Muleshoe for a while. She's looking for a pilot to fly her outta here."

Six of the bar's patrons stepped forward, but Burdy held up his gnarled hand and shook his head. "The first guy to offer Miz Kincaid a ride will have to answer to me and Joe Brennan."

The six stepped back, their expressions clouded with disappointment, but their interest barely quelled. Perrie shifted nervously and glanced at Burdy.

"And she ain't here lookin' for a husband, either, so you all can stop your gawkin' and get back to your fun."

"I'm perfectly able to speak for myself," she said as Burdy drew her along toward a table.

He gallantly pulled out the red vinyl chair for her, then helped her out of her parka. "'Course, you'll be expected to dance with them," Burdy said, once he'd seated himself across from her and settled his imaginary dog at his feet.

Her gaze snapped up from the menu to his face. "What?"

"Well now, that's only common courtesy up here. They can't dance with each other, and when there's a woman about, they don't waste much time. I expect you'll get twirled around the floor more times than you'll be able to count. If you're lucky, the brides will stop by and reduce your odds of gettin' dizzy."

Burdy had no more said the words when the front door of Doyle's swung open and three women stepped inside. Perrie wouldn't have known there were women behind the parka hoods and scarves except that the conversation stopped again and every man in the place turned to look. "That's them," he said. "They're a promisin' lot. Better than the first three."

"There were three others?"

"Yep. The boys placed the ad down in Los Angeles. I guess they thought they might get lucky and nab themselves a movie star or one of them supermodels. Those three girls lasted about a week before Joe had to fly them out. They just weren't cut out for the cold. But these three—I got my money on at least two of 'em stayin'."

Perrie watched them slip out of their coats and take their places at a table. They looked like normal, intelligent women to her. All three were attractive in their own different ways and, from what she could see, ranged in age from midtwenties to early thirties. "What about their grooms?" she asked. "Aren't they going to get mad if someone dances with their girls?"

"It don't work that way. The boys that paid in get the chance to go through the letters and choose the girls. But once they're up here, it's pretty much a free-for-all. The man who woos 'er wins 'er fair and square."

"That doesn't seem fair to me. What about the men who didn't pay?"

"Well, there ain't many single men that didn't get in

on it. There's me...and Paddy. He's still pinin' over the wife he lost a few years back. And there's Ralphie Simpson. He's been married and divorced five times so he don't want any part of a woman bent on marriage. And that's it, except for Joe Brennan and Hawk."

"Every unmarried man in town except for you and the other four is looking for a bride?"

"That's about it."

She glanced over the top of her menu at Burdy. "So, what's the story with Brennan? How come he isn't in on the bride deal?"

Burdy scratched his chin as he pondered her question for a long moment. "I don't rightly know. I 'spect he likes bein' a lone wolf. Though there ain't a shortage of ladies lookin' to put an end to that. They all say he's a real charmer, knows exactly how to treat 'em. They're always talking about his eyes, though I can't figure what's so special about 'em."

"His eyes? I don't see anything remarkable about his eyes, either," Perrie lied. "And as for charming...well, he certainly isn't my type."

"You know, he rescued a purdy thing off Denali just a few days back. Plucked her right off the mountain and saved her life. He's a helluva pilot, too."

Perrie's interest was aroused and she leaned forward. "Really? He didn't mention that."

"He don't brag on himself much. But everybody likes him. He's generous to a fault. Last winter, he flew Addie Pruett out when her ma fell ill. She didn't have the money to pay for the flight, so Joe told her she could do his laundry for three months in exchange. And he brings me fresh vegetables for my fire hall feeds without charging me for the freight. I 'spect he don't charge me full price for the produce, either, but I don't have proof of that."

Perrie's journalistic instincts kicked into overdrive. "What did he do in Seattle?"

A shrug was all Burdy had for that question. The old man cocked his head in the direction of the bar. "Why don't you ask him yourself? He's sittin' over there at the end of the bar. He's been watchin' you since we sat down."

She turned to look and found Joe Brennan leaning back against the bar, his pale eyes fixed on her with another disconcerting gaze. For an instant, she thought of looking away, of avoiding his direct stare. But instead, she tipped her chin up and gave him a little wave. His only response was an oh-so-subtle lift of his eyebrow before he turned to talk to the man next to him.

For the first time since she'd met him, he wasn't wearing a cap. His thick dark hair brushed the collar of his flannel shirt and fell in a boyish shock across his forehead, careless and incredibly sexy. His sleeves were rolled up to his elbows and her gaze drifted along smooth, muscular arms and strong, capable hands. She noticed how his jeans hugged narrow hips and long legs when he hooked his heel on the foot rail. No doubt about it. Joe Brennan filled out a pair of jeans better than any man she'd ever met.

"You fancy him?"

She twisted around at Burdy's question. "What? No. Why would you think that?"

Burdy shrugged, a grin quirking the deep grooves around his mouth. "Haven't met a lady yet that could resist him. And you seem interested."

"I'm a reporter," she snapped. "Learning deep dark secrets about people is what I'm good at." Perrie leaned back in her chair. "And I'll wager you dinner tonight that I can find out what Joe Brennan did in Seattle before he came here."

"I'd take you up on it, but Joe said you don't have any money."

She frowned. Burdy was right. How was she supposed to live here in Muleshoe without a penny to her name? Milt had stolen all her money, had forced her into exile. Did he expect her to starve, as well. "You're right. I don't have any money."

"Not for gamblin'. But Joe said your boss gave him the okay to pay your way around town. Paddy'll run a tab and so will Louise Weller down at the general store."

"Well, if I choose to wager a dinner here or there, Milt Freeman can damn well pay for it," Perrie said. Her chair scraped on the rough wood floor and she stood up. "This will take me about five minutes. You can order the cheeseburger plate and a beer for me while I'm gone."

She fixed her gaze on Joe Brennan's wide, flannel-covered shoulders and headed across the room. But she'd barely gotten five feet before a beefy man with a thick black beard stepped in front of her.

He cleared his throat and she watched a blush creep up his cheeks. "Miz Kincaid. My name's Luther Paulson. I'd be obliged if you'd take a turn around the dance floor with me."

Perrie opened her mouth to refuse, but the poor man looked so nervous that she didn't have the heart. She smiled weakly and nodded. "All right. A dance would be nice. But just one."

"I wouldn't impose myself on you for any more," Luther said, his expression brightening.

True to his word, Luther didn't ask for a second dance. Nor did George Koslowski, Erv Saunders or the

other three single men who came along after them to
claim just one turn around the dance floor. She'd tried to
remember their names, but after the third, they all became one big blur of facial hair and flannel. And the
three brides hadn't fared any better, for they were out on
the dance floor with her the whole time, chatting amia-
bly with their partners.

She finally pleaded thirst and at least four men
jumped to buy her a beer. But she waved them off and
made her way to the bar through the crowd of hopefuls
that surrounded the dance floor, refusing more invita-
tions along the way.

The stool beside Joe Brennan was empty now, as were
almost all the stools, the former occupants now cluttered
around the dance floor hoping for a shot at a female
partner. She slid in beside him, sending him a sideways
glance.

He smiled. "You're a popular lady tonight," he said.
He didn't look her way, merely stared into his mug of
beer.

"Not so popular," she said. "You didn't ask me to
dance."

He chuckled, then took a long swallow of his beer. He
set the empty mug on the bar and turned to her. "Those
men out there have a reason for dancing with you and
it's pretty serious business. I'm not one to stand in their
way."

"And I suppose you can't think of one reason you
might have to ask me to dance?"

"Oh, I could think of a few," he said. "But then, I've
got more than a few reasons *not* to dance with you, Kincaid."

"And what might those be, Brennan?"

"Well, beyond the fact that you'd talk my ear off and

try once again to get me to take you back to Seattle, I also might be thinking that it would give you the wrong kind of ideas about me."

Perrie slowly nodded. "You're worried about what I said earlier. About you wanting to kiss me. Well, I won't hold that against you, Brennan. I've been fully informed of your reputation with the ladies." She reached over and grabbed his arm. "Come on, then. If you won't ask me, I'll have to ask you."

He growled softly in protest, but turned and followed her out to the dance floor. Perrie expected more of the same clumsy embarrassment that she'd had from her other partners. But Joe slipped his arm around her waist and pulled her effortlessly into his arms. He moved with the music, as if he'd been dancing all his life, and suddenly she was the one who felt clumsy and uneasy.

Her breath caught in her throat as his hand splayed across her shoulders, then slowly slipped toward the small of her back. His touch sent a tingle down her spine, and for a moment, her knees went soft. "You dance very well," she murmured, fixing her attention on his chest, avoiding his eyes once again.

"Surprised?"

"Maybe," she conceded. "So what's your story, Brennan?"

"My story?"

She looked up at him, now that she'd managed to start breathing again. "Yeah, what brought you up here to live in the Great White North? Burdy says you used to live in Seattle until about five years ago."

"Have you and Burdy been gossiping about me?"

"We were talking about the brides and the subject turned in your direction. He couldn't tell me much more. He says you're a crackerjack pilot, though."

He lifted a dark eyebrow. "I do all right. I haven't lost a passenger yet, although I was sorely tempted earlier today."

"Then you're fearless?"

Joe chuckled. "We have a saying here in Alaska, Kincaid. There are bold pilots and there are old pilots. But there are no old, bold pilots."

Perrie smiled. "I like that. So, who were you before you became a bush pilot, Brennan? And how do you know Milt Freeman?"

He stared over her shoulder for a long moment as if contemplating what he was going to tell her. But then he shrugged. "I had a job like most folks do. I sat behind a desk and pushed papers." He glanced down and met her gaze. "I'm afraid it's a rather boring story for a woman like you, Kincaid."

She narrowed her gaze. "And I'm afraid I don't believe you, Brennan. You forget that I've got a nose for a story and I smell one right now. Milt mentioned that you owed him a favor or two. For what?"

"Let's not talk. I thought you wanted to dance."

His voice was warm, persuasive. A little too persuasive for Perrie's taste. "Did you and Milt meet up here or did you know each other back in Seattle?"

"Were you born a reporter, Kincaid?"

"Actually, I was. From the time I was a little kid, I wanted my own newspaper. In fact, I used to publish a little neighborhood journal called the *Honey Acres Gazette*. I wrote the stories and drew the pictures and I made ten copies and passed them out to the kids in the neighborhood. I was the one who broke the story about the stray cat living in the culvert under Mrs. Moriarty's driveway."

"You are quite a woman, Kincaid." He chuckled, then

pulled her closer. At first, the feel of his long, lean body pressed against hers was too much to take. Her pulse quickened and her mind whirled. But then, as they danced, she realized that she enjoyed the crazy sensations racing through her body.

That's the key, Perrie thought to herself. *Don't fight it, enjoy it...but not too much*. She cleared her throat. "Well, I told you about myself, now why don't you spill your guts, Brennan?"

"I'm not going to answer your questions. If you want to write yourself a story, why don't you write the one Milt gave you? About the brides."

She rolled her eyes. "The brides are easy. I need a challenge and I think I've found one. You're going to be sorry you didn't fly me back to Seattle, Brennan, especially if you're keeping any secrets."

He yanked her closer, his arm tightening around her waist until she could do nothing but allow her body to mold itself against his. Every thought in her head took flight again as her hips rubbed against his, as her hand skimmed along his muscular arm and her fingers folded against his palm. A flood of warmth seeped into her cheeks as her mind wandered to other aspects of Joe Brennan's anatomy.

But her speculation was cut short when Paddy Doyle appeared beside them. "Sorry to interrupt," he said, wiping his hands on his apron, "but Louise Weller just called here looking for you, Joe. She says little Wally was shoveling snow off the roof and he fell. She thinks he may have broken his leg."

Joe loosened his grip and she took the opportunity to step back a bit. As she did, his hands slipped from her body and a sliver of regret shot through her. She fought the temptation to step closer again, to place his hands where they'd once been. Instead, she risked a glance up at Joe, but he seemed unaffected by the break in their physical contact.

His jaw tightened, then he ran his fingers through his hair. "I swear, that boy has broken more bones than he's got in his body. His dad's insurance company's damn near paid for my plane."

Paddy nodded. "She's put a splint on it and said she'll meet you out at the airstrip."

"We've got weather and it's getting dark. I don't know if I'm going to be able to get him out." He turned and walked off the dance floor, his thoughts now occupied with more important matters.

Perrie followed after him, stumbling in the oversize boots. She snatched up her jacket from the chair across from Burdy, then grabbed the cold cheeseburger. "I'm going with you, Brennan."

He spun around, almost as if he'd forgotten she was there. He sighed and shook his head. "Give it up, Kincaid. You're staying right here. You're safe and I intend to keep you that way." He looked at Burdy. "Keep an eye on her, will you?"

Burdy nodded. With that, Joe grabbed his jacket and his cap and stalked out the door. Perrie watched him leave, his words echoing in her head. Her heart skipped and a smile twitched at her lips. It was kind of nice having someone care about her safety, especially a man as sexy and compelling as Joe Brennan. The notion made her feel all warm and gooey inside.

Perrie blinked, her silly fantasies grinding to a halt. Scowling, she shoved her hands into her jean pockets then turned back to the table where Burdy and her dinner waited.

"Get a grip, Kincaid," she muttered to herself. "Going

soft in the head for Joe Brennan is not going to get you out of Muleshoe and back to Seattle." She pulled out her chair and sat down, tossing her jacket on the floor.

As she silently munched on the cold cheeseburger, she let her mind wander back to Joe Brennan. An idea slowly formed in her mind, and as it crystalized, a laugh bubbled out of her throat. Why hadn't she thought of it before? It was all so simple.

She knew exactly how to get back to civilization! And as soon as Joe Brennan returned from Fairbanks, she'd put her new plan into action.

"I'M PRETTY SURE it's broke," Burdy said, scampering ahead of Joe on the snow-packed path to Perrie's cabin, his movements quick and nervous.

"What the hell happened? She was fine when I left last night."

"She says she slipped on a patch of ice and fell walkin' to the outhouse in the dark. I shoulda been there. A lady like Miz Kincaid ain't used to the weather here. They don't have ice in Seattle. And them boots I gave her are a couple sizes too big."

Joe frowned, a slow suspicion growing in his mind. "You weren't there when she fell?"

Burdy shook his head. "I'm sorry, Joe. I know you tol' me to watch her, but a man cain't stay with a gal like that twenty-four hours. It wouldn't be seemly." The old man gave Joe a solemn look. "People might talk."

A smile quirked Joe's lips as an image of Burdy and Perrie, caught in a romantic tryst, flashed in his mind. "I'm not blaming you, Burdy. In fact, I'd be willing to bet that Perrie Kincaid is up to something. She'd do just about anything to get out of Muleshoe."

"You mean to say that little gal broke her wrist on purpose?"

Joe took the front steps of Perrie's cabin two at a time. "No, I don't think her wrist is broken at all. I think she's faking, Burdy, and I'm about to prove it."

Gathering his resolve, he knocked at the front door, then pushed it open. He caught a brief glimpse of Perrie before she scrambled back into bed and pulled the covers up to her chin. Burdy waited on the porch, carrying on a low dialogue with Strike. By the time Joe closed the door behind him, she was beneath the quilts, her right arm clutched to her chest.

She looked so small and frail, tucked into the huge iron bed. Her auburn hair was mussed, falling in disarray around her face. For an instant, he felt a small measure of delight in seeing her again. But then he quickly smothered the feeling as he realized that it would have meant he had actually missed her. Hell, he barely knew her.

He crossed the room in three long strides, composing an expression of deep concern on his face. When Joe reached the bed, he slowly sat down on the edge. Her wince at the movement told him that either Perrie really had hurt herself—or she was a consummate actress. He was willing to wager on the latter.

Reaching out, he gently brushed her hair from her forehead, ignoring the flood of heat that seeped into his fingertips and set his nerves on fire. "What happened?" he asked, his voice soft with feigned worry. "Burdy says you hurt your wrist."

"I—I think it's just sprained. Nothing to worry about. It—it'll be fine in a few days."

Joe hid a smile. So she was trying to turn the tables on him. "But it could be broken." He reached out and took her forearm in his hands. Her wrist was limp and he wove his fingers through hers to test the joint. His mind instantly focused on her hand, so smooth and soft in his. A lady's hand. Long, delicate fingers that might drive him mad with— Joe cleared his throat and blinked hard.

"Do you really think it could be broken?" Her words were soft and breathy and he glanced up to meet her wide green eyes.

The intensity of her gaze rocked him, yet he couldn't draw his eyes from hers. "I'm not sure," he said, leaning closer. "What do you think?"

He could feel her breath soft on his face, quick and shallow, as if his nearness made her uneasy. "It really does hurt," she offered. She added another wince for good measure.

Joe let his gaze drift down to her mouth. Suddenly all thought of catching her in her lie slipped from his mind. He found himself transfixed by her lips and he leaned forward and brushed his mouth against hers.

A tiny moan escaped her and he deepened his kiss, savoring the taste of her. He'd thought a lot about kissing her in the hours since he'd left Muleshoe, many more times than he'd care to admit. But he'd never imagined it would be as good as it was.

Perrie Kincaid knew just how to kiss a man, how to tease and tantalize with barely an effort. Her mouth moved gently under his and tiny sounds rose from her throat, urging him on. Her fingers slowly splayed across his chest and slipped up inside his down jacket until they twined through his hair at the nape of his—

Her fingers. Joe's thoughts came back into sharp focus and his mouth curved beneath the onslaught of hers. "I don't believe it's broken," he murmured, letting his lips slide down to her throat.

"Hmm?"

Slowly, he reached back and grabbed her hands, unwinding her arms from around his neck. Dazed by what had passed between them, she stared at him, uncomprehending. "I said, I don't think your wrist is broken." He held her arm out in front of her and shook it until her hand flopped back and forth. "I'm not a doctor, but I'd say your wrist is just fine. It even looks like that sprain cleared up pretty quick. Maybe it was the kiss."

Slowly her eyes cleared and her confusion was replaced with anger. Anger at him, and at herself for falling into his trap. She sputtered, then cursed softly. "You did that on purpose."

Joe lifted his eyebrow. "What?"

"You know what! You—you kissed me. Distracted me."

"And you kissed me," he countered. "And I do believe you enjoyed it. Enough to forget your little plan to get me to evac you out to the hospital in Fairbanks, Kincaid."

She shoved him aside and crawled out of bed, then began to pace the room. Every few seconds, she shot him a frustrated glare before returning to her pacing. "I can't believe this," she muttered. "I'm trapped here. There's no way out. No one cares that I've got a huge story to break back home." She stopped and braced her hands on her hips. "Do you have any idea how important this is?"

"Important enough to get killed for?" Joe asked. "No story is that important."

Perrie opened her mouth to reply, then snapped it shut. For a long moment, she was silent. "What do you care?"

Strangely enough, he did care. The more time he spent

with Perrie Kincaid, the more he cared what happened to her. But the hell if he was about to tell her that. "Milt Freeman cares. And I owe him a favor. So, whether I want to or not, I have to care."

"What kind of favor?" she challenged.

"He saved my life." Joe wasn't sure why he chose to tell her that, though he wasn't prepared to explain himself further. Maybe he'd hoped that she'd see how determined he was and forget about leaving Muleshoe. But he could see from her expression that he'd only kindled her curiosity.

"And when was that?" she asked.

Joe shook his head. "That is none of your business. Now, if you've recovered sufficiently, I've got work to do. I'd suggest you go into town with Burdy. He's got to get ready for the spaghetti feed and you can shop for groceries. You're going to be here for a while."

Turning on his heel, he headed toward the door, satisfied that he'd finally put an end to all her escape plans. Whether he liked it or not, he was stuck with her.

"Just wait one minute, Captain Charm," she called. "I'd like to discuss the plumbing situation with you."

Joe braced his arm against the doorjamb, refusing to turn back and face her. "And what might that situation be?"

She stalked across the room and placed herself between him and the door. "Where the hell is my bathroom? Burdy has me traipsing through the snow to a damn outhouse."

"You should be satisfied with running water," Joe replied. "Most folks in town still get their water from the town's well house."

"I demand a cabin with indoor facilities."

He gently pushed her aside and opened the cabin

door. "You've got hot water. And there's a tub on the back porch. You drag it inside and fill it. Or you can take a sauna with me and Burdy and Hawk every night if that's too much work."

She followed him out onto the porch. "And you consider this civilization?"

"We discuss all manner of subjects during our saunas. Philosophy, literature, politics. You'd be surprised."

"I'm not talking about your conversations. I'm talking about toilets."

Joe turned to face her, meeting her angry gaze. "This is Alaska, Kincaid," he said in an even voice, fighting the urge to soften the hard line of her lips with his mouth. "It's supposed to be rugged. That's part of the experience. I told you it was a tough place, especially for a woman."

He expected her to make another plea for escape. After all, she hadn't chosen to come to Alaska of her own free will. She'd been coerced into coming and he really couldn't blame her for being uncomfortable with the amenities—or lack of them. But Perrie surprised him by bracing her hands on her hips, a stubborn expression suffusing her flushed and angry features.

"Just what are you saying? That I'm not tough enough for Alaska?"

Joe shrugged, disarmed by her mercurial moods. "You're the one who's whining about the plumbing. Now, if there's nothing else, I've got a flight to make." She opened her mouth to protest, but he held up his hand. "No, I'm not taking you with me."

"That's not what I was going to say!" she shouted as he strode down the path. "If you can live without indoor plumbing, I can, too."

"Good," Joe shouted over his shoulder, "because you don't have much choice."

Burdy caught up to him halfway back to the main lodge. He fell into step beside Joe, then gave him a sideways glance. "I don't s'pose yer plannin' to tell her that there's indoor facilities in the lodge?"

"And have her move in with me and Hawk?"

"There's an empty room until Sammy and Julia and Tanner come back for the summer."

Joe stopped and shot Burdy a disbelieving look. "Would *you* want to live with her?"

"Well, she really didn't choose to come up here. You could make her life a little more comfortable," Burdy suggested.

"There's no room in the lodge for guests. Tanner and his new family are coming back in a few days. And you know what happened when Julia set foot inside the lodge. I'm not willing to take any chances."

Burdy chuckled. "I expect that you and Hawk will meet your match before long." He paused and grinned. "Maybe you already have?"

Joe sighed. "Don't you start on me. I've got enough on my mind trying to run Polar Bear Air. With Tanner involved with his wife and new son, he hasn't been much help here at the lodge. And Hawk is long overdue for one of his disappearing acts."

"Then why don't you jest do as the lady asks and take her back to Seattle? Must be a pretty big debt you owe her boss."

"Why don't you mind your own business," Joe growled.

Burdy shook his head and whistled for Strike. When the imaginary dog reached his side, he leaned down and patted him on the head. "Seems to me yer protestin' a little too loudly."

With that, the old man took off toward the lodge, muttering to Strike as he walked.

Joe pulled off his cap and ran his fingers through his hair. Truth was, he'd love to return the woman right back to where she came from, but Joe Brennan didn't welch on his debts. He owed Milt Freeman his life and he wasn't about to let his friend down.

Even if it meant putting up with Perrie Kincaid for another few weeks.

4

PERRIE STOOD on the front porch of the brides' house. She pushed the hood of her parka back, then fumbled out of the oversize mittens Burdy had lent her. She'd been in Alaska for four days and already she was climbing the walls. She could only spend so much time wandering around her cabin and eating breakfast, lunch and dinner at Doyle's. Either she'd eat herself into oblivion or she'd go stark raving mad from cabin fever.

The only choice left was to follow Milt's orders and write his blasted story about the mail-order brides. It would take her about an hour to interview the subjects and another few hours to put the story together. Considering her own feelings about marital commitment, she could at least offer a completely unbiased viewpoint.

There had never been much time in her life for men beyond a few passionate, short-term flings. It wasn't that she didn't want to be part of some man's life. She liked men—well-read men with interesting careers, charming men with clever smiles and deep blue eyes.

An image of Joe Brennan drifted through her thoughts and she pinched her eyes shut and tried to will it away. Yes, Joe Brennan was attractive. And if he wasn't so set on making her life miserable, she might consider him more than just a convenient outlet for her frustration. But when push came to shove, he was probably like all the other men she'd known. He would never be able to put up with her life—the late hours, the broken dates, her single-minded devotion to her work. And he lived in Alaska.

To be honest, after a few months with a man, she usually found herself a little bored. As a reporter, she prided herself on her ability to learn everything about a person in a very short time. Unfortunately, once she learned all she could, there was little else to talk about. A once promising relationship usually fizzled in short order. The only reason she had the slightest interest in Joe Brennan was because she hadn't been able to crack that roguish facade of his and bend him to her will.

Perrie sighed. Whoever said women could "have it all" didn't have a clue as to what it took to be a top-notch investigative reporter. She had resigned herself long ago to never "having it all." She wasn't even sure she wanted it all, considering that "all" just took too much energy to have.

A devoted husband and a loving family were fine for other women, but not for Perrie Kincaid. She had taken another road long ago, made choices that required a near solitary pursuit of her dreams. She couldn't go back and change her mind. She'd come too far. This was all she had—her work—and she was happy with that choice.

She knocked on the door, and a few moments later it swung open and she was greeted by the warm but hesitant smile of a slender blonde, one of the trio from the bar. "You're that woman visiting from Seattle, aren't you?" the woman asked.

Perrie shouldn't be surprised. Talk would travel around a small town like this quickly. She held out her hand. "Hi, I'm Perrie Kincaid from the *Seattle Star*. I've been sent here to interview you and the other mail-order brides. May I come in?" She didn't wait for an invitation, just shook the woman's hand firmly then slipped past her into the cozy warmth of the cabin. Experience had told her that confidence went further than manners when it came to getting a story.

She slowly strolled around the main room of the cabin, making a mental inventory of her surroundings. A few descriptive phrases to set the scene added color to human interest stories. The cabin was much larger than hers, boasting separate bedrooms and a variety of modern conveniences. She nearly moaned out loud when she pushed open the bathroom door and came upon a shower and a toilet.

"My name is Linda Sorenson," the woman said. "I must say, I was startled to find a woman at the door. All our guests have been men."

"I can imagine," Perrie murmured, recalling the scene at Doyle's. "I'm here to write a follow-up to the original story published in our paper." She stopped to stand in front of the fire. When her hands were warmed sufficiently, she turned and faced her subject. "This is a very nice cabin. There are three of you living here?"

Linda smiled, then rearranged the magazines on a scarred coffee table. "The others are out back. Would you like a cup of coffee?"

Perrie couldn't help but put aside her professional demeanor. Linda seemed so friendly, and right now she could use all the allies she could find, since Brennan had most of Muleshoe watching her every move. Maybe the three brides could offer some help in her escape plans. "Sure," she said with a smile, pulling her notepad from her pocket before she slipped out of her jacket. "I'm having trouble adjusting to the cold so anything warm would do." She made a few notes and waited until

Linda returned from the kitchen with the coffee, then sat down across from her on the sofa.

Linda smoothed her palms along her legs. "What would you like to know?"

"Why don't you tell me why you decided to come to Alaska?" Perrie asked after taking a sip of her coffee.

Linda took a deep breath then let it out slowly. "It's hard to explain without sounding a little silly. Do you believe in destiny, Miss Kincaid?"

Perrie glanced over the rim of her mug. "Destiny?"

"One day, I was looking through the newspaper. I rarely have time to read the paper. I'm a nurse and my schedule is rather hectic. But I had time that day and I saw the ad for brides. I knew that I had to come to Alaska. I just felt as if something—or someone—was waiting for me here."

Perrie sighed inwardly. It did sound a little silly. "Actually, I'm not a big proponent of destiny. I think a person determines their own future. Fate doesn't have anything to do with it."

"Have you ever been in love, Miss Kincaid?"

Perrie paused, not sure how—or whether—to answer the question. What did her love life have to do with the story she was writing? She was the one asking the questions. Besides, she wasn't sure she wanted a complete stranger to know that Perrie Kincaid, a highly intelligent thirty-three-year-old woman, wasn't even sure what love was.

"Why don't we stick to your story?" she said lightly. "Why are you so sure you want to get married?"

"Because I know I'd be really good at it. I want someone to share my life with, I want to fall in love and have children and grow old with a good man."

"And you expect to find that man here in Alaska?"

"Why not? He could be here. The odds are good."

Perrie smiled. "But the goods are kind of odd, don't you think? Besides, how do you know your destiny isn't waiting for you in Newfoundland?"

Linda smiled. "Well, if I don't find him here, I'll just have to keep looking."

"There are other things in life besides marriage, aren't there?"

"Sure there are. And I'm not necessarily set on marriage. But I'm never going to give up on finding love."

Perrie considered her words for a long moment. Was she missing something here? She'd never considered love very important at all. In fact, she considered men more trouble than they were worth. Was that because she could put such a crazy emotion in perspective? Or was it because she'd never come close to feeling that emotion?

"So you hope to find love here in Muleshoe? And what will you do if that happens? Are you going to give up your career in Seattle and move up here?"

Linda smiled. "I don't know. That's what's so exciting about this whole thing. I'm not really sure what's going to happen until it does. I'm enjoying the journey as much as the destination."

Perrie stared down at her notepad. All of this sappy stuff was not going to make a story, unless she was writing it for one of those romance magazines. She glanced around the room, then back at Linda. A long silence grew between them, broken suddenly by the sound of the front door opening.

The other two brides stumbled inside, laughing, their jackets covered with snow. Perrie stood and watched as they tugged off hats and mittens. They both turned to her and regarded her with curiosity until Linda stood and made the introductions.

The tiny brunette, Allison Keifer, spoke first. "I didn't know we were going to be interviewed again. We would have been here earlier but we've been practicing."

"You have to practice finding a husband?" Perrie asked, leaning forward. Maybe there was something to this story.

"No," Mary Ellen Davenport replied, giggling. She was a prettily plump woman with pale brown hair and a sparkling smile. "We're practicing for the Muleshoe Games. They're having a brides' competition next weekend, on Valentine's Day. We compete in all sorts of things—snowshoeing, dogsledding, wood chopping."

"I suppose it's so these men can see what kind of wives we'll make," Allison said. "But we're just going to have fun. And there's a nice prize for the winner. A weekend up at the resort at Cooper Hot Springs. Everything's included, the room, the flight, the—"

"The flight?" Perrie asked. "Someone's going to fly the winner out of Muleshoe?"

Linda nodded. "And after the games, there's a dance at Doyle's. Are you interested? The brides' competition is open to any single woman."

Another plan began to form in Perrie's mind. She could train with the brides and win the event and at the same time get a nice angle on the story. And once she escaped Muleshoe, she'd be able to find her way back to Seattle and finish a story that really mattered. "Sure," Perrie said. "I think I'd like to enter the games. Tell me more."

"You'll need to practice if you want to win," Mary Ellen said. "There are a few single women from town who are entering. Ringers, I say. They'll be tough to beat. You can practice with us."

"Or you can get one of those dishy bachelors from Bachelor Creek Lodge to help you," Allison teased. "You're staying there, aren't you?"

Perrie nodded.

"Lucky girl."

Perrie arched her eyebrow. "Lucky?"

"That's bachelor central. Three of the dreamiest guys in Alaska and they live up there."

"If you're counting Burdy as a bachelor dreamboat, you've definitely been in the wilderness too long."

"Oh, no. Not that Burdy fellow. I'm talking about Joe Brennan and Kyle Hawkins. And there's another one, but he just got married—Tanner is his name, I think. Linda had a date with Joe Brennan the night we arrived here."

Perrie tried to look indifferent but her interest was piqued. Leaning forward, she asked, "He didn't waste much time, did he?"

"He took Allison out the night after that," Linda countered.

"He asked me out, too," Mary Ellen admitted, "but I had a previous engagement."

"He was really charming, but not the marrying type," Linda commented.

"Charming," Perrie repeated.

"He's just so sweet and attentive," Linda continued. "And funny. And cute, too. He has this way about him. It's hard to explain, but it makes you want to tear off his clothes and drag him into bed."

"Mel Gibson eyes," Mary Ellen observed.

"A little boy in the body of a man," Allison added.

"But definitely scared of commitment. A one-date wonder."

"Then you both went to..." Perrie couldn't finish the question, a strange surge of jealousy stopping her words.

"Of course not!" Linda cried.

"Though I was tempted," Allison added. "Those eyes of his could melt a girl's panties."

Perrie scolded herself silently. What right did she have to be jealous? Or envious? She'd pegged Joe Brennan as a ladies' man from the moment she'd met him. A confirmed bachelor who used his charm and good looks to make women weak in the knees and breathless with adoration. Even she hadn't been immune.

At least she was smart enough to see Brennan for what he was. And clever enough to keep her distance. Though it hadn't been too hard, considering she hadn't seen much of him lately.

Linda laughed. "It took Allison about three days to evaluate every bachelor within a twenty-mile radius. She's got this down to a science."

"I believe in being thorough," Allison said. "After all, I'm the one who has to look at him across the dinner table. I only want the best."

"The only one she can't figure out is Hawk," Linda teased.

Perrie glanced up from her notes. "Kyle Hawkins? Brennan's partner?"

"They call him Hawk. And he's the only man who hasn't said a single word to her," Mary Ellen said. "He reminds me of Gregory Peck in that old movie...I can't remember the name."

"Mary Ellen never remembers the names of movies.

And if you ask me, that Hawk is a little too quiet," Linda said. "Maybe he's hiding a tortured soul."

"I haven't met him yet," Perrie admitted. "I'm not sure I want to. Brennan is enough to deal with."

"You're a reporter," Allison said. "Find out all about him and then tell us."

Perrie slowly closed her notepad. "I'll make you a deal," she said with a conspiratorial grin. "You teach me how to chop wood and walk on snowshoes and drive a dogsled, and I'll report back on the mysterious Mr. Hawk."

Mary Ellen giggled. "This is going to be so much fun! Just like that old movie where the three girls go to Rome and find love. The one with the fountain? Only this is Alaska and there are four of us...and no fountain."

"I'm not in this to find a husband," Perrie quickly explained. "All I'm interested in is the trip out of Muleshoe."

JOE PULLED THE FRONT DOOR of the lodge closed and dropped his sunglasses over his eyes against the sun-drenched snow. The days were getting longer and the bitter cold that had marked all of January was beginning to release its grip. It would be months until the river broke up and spring came, but they were halfway through winter now and there was an end in sight.

A curse split the silent air and he turned and glanced up at Perrie's cabin. He'd spent the past five days flying supplies into the bush and hadn't had time to check on how she was doing. She and Burdy had become friends and the old guy had taken her into town for meals, but beyond that, Perrie Kincaid had been keeping herself busy with her own activities.

To tell the truth, she wasn't nearly as much trouble as

he first thought she'd be. She'd obviously come to the conclusion that there was no way she'd be able to get out of Muleshoe and had decided to make the best of her free time. He casually strolled up the path toward the cabins, a satisfied smile curling his lips. He had won this little battle between the two of them and he couldn't wait to gloat.

As the cabin came into view, he caught sight of Perrie, lying in the snow, her feet up in the air. A stab of concern pierced his mind and he wondered if she'd really injured herself this time. But then he noticed she was wearing snowshoes.

"Hey!" he called. "Are you all right?"

Perrie turned over on her side and regarded him with thinly veiled hostility. Her hair was caked in snow and her face was wet. She looked as if she had taken a header into a snowbank. "Go away!" she cried. "Leave me alone!"

Joe stood over her and couldn't help but laugh. She looked so darn cute, all covered with snow and ready to explode with anger. "What the hell are you doing?" he asked, holding out his hand to yank her to her feet. He turned her around and brushed the snow off her backside. It wasn't until he'd pulled his hand away that he realized how intimate the contact actually had been.

"I'm practicing," Perrie said, twisting away from him and finishing the job herself.

"Falling into the snow?"

"No, Mr. Smarty Britches, snowshoeing. It's just that these things are so big, and I'm supposed to try to move as fast as I can, but my feet get all tangled up. It's like running in swim flippers."

"Why do you have to move fast?" He paused, then held up his hand to stop her reply. "Let me guess. I assume you aren't planning to run a footrace with a stampeding moose, so I'm going to have to surmise that you've decided to walk to Fairbanks?"

She tried to move away from him, but one of her snowshoes caught the edge of the other and she began to lose her balance again. He reached out and grabbed her elbow, but as soon as she righted herself, she pushed him away. "I'm going to enter the Muleshoe Games next weekend. And I'm going to win that trip to Cooper Hot Springs. And once I do, I'll be out of Muleshoe for good."

Joe laughed, the sound echoing through the silent woods. "You're going to win the brides' competition? You're not even a bride-to-be."

Perrie bristled. "I'm a single woman. And I'm a reasonably fit individual. I work out...sometimes. You don't think I can win?"

"Not a chance, Kincaid."

Perrie bent down and fumbled with the leather straps on the snowshoes. She lost her balance again and tumbled back into the snow, but this time he didn't help her up. She wrestled with the snowshoes until she'd managed to pull both of them off, then scrambled to her feet. "You just watch me," she said, her chin tipped up defiantly. "I've been practicing splitting wood and I'm getting pretty damn good at it. I've actually hit the log twice with the ax and I've only been practicing for an hour."

She stalked around the side of the cabin and returned with an ax and a log as if to prove her point. He watched her push the log into a snowdrift before she hefted the ax up on her shoulder.

"Be careful with that," he warned. "Should you be doing that with your sore arm?"

"My arm is fine. Besides, I know what I'm doing."

"You should set that up on top of a harder surface be-fore you—"

"I don't need any advice from you!" Perrie snapped, raising the ax.

Joe watched as she brought the ax over her head. But he could see that her aim was seriously off. Instead, she swung to the right of the wood and buried the ax in the snowdrift, continuing down until the blade hit rock be-neath the snow.

"Eeeoow!" she cried, snatching her hands back, stung by the impact. She jumped up and down and rubbed her palms together, her eyes watering with the pain. Finally, unable to handle the ache, she sat down in the snow.

"I told you—"

"Oh, zip it!"

Joe grinned and sat down across from her, then reached out and pulled off her mittens, then his gloves. Slowly, he rubbed her fingers between his hands, work-ing his way up through her palms to her wrists. "There's a rock border all around this porch."

"Thanks for warning me."

"It feels worse in the cold."

Her fingers were warm against his, tiny and delicate. Her nails were trimmed short and unpolished. He wouldn't have expected a perfect manicure from a woman as practical as Perrie, especially since she didn't wear a lot of makeup, either.

She had a natural beauty all her own. Her ivory skin, now touched with pink from the cold, was perfectly smooth. Impossibly long lashes framed her clear green eyes. And her mouth, that wide mouth with those lush lips. He'd found his attention drawn to her mouth again and again, remembering the kiss they'd shared.

His gaze lingered on her mouth for a long moment. "Is that better?" he murmured.

She didn't answer and he looked up into her eyes to catch her staring at him. He wasn't sure what came over him, but the next thing he knew, he bent forward and covered her lips with his. She fell back into the snow and Joe stretched his body over hers, groaning at the feel of her soft form beneath his.

He rolled her over in the snow, pulling her on top of him and holding her face between his palms, afraid that she might break their kiss before he was ready. But she seemed to have no intention of pulling away.

Gently, he explored her mouth with his tongue, tasting and teasing. For an instant, rational thought returned and he wondered just what he was doing rolling around in the snow with a woman who wanted nothing more than to make him look like a fool.

But the truth be told, Joe liked the way she kissed. She didn't go all soft and breathless in his arms, but instead she kissed him as if she were truly enjoying the experience. He'd never known a woman who had tempted him so sorely, yet managed to drive him crazy at the same time. She was a challenge, and Joe never walked away from a challenge.

He pulled her beneath him once more, his lips never leaving hers, an intimate contact that he didn't want to break. His mind swam with images of her and he couldn't help but draw back and look down at her.

Her eyes were closed and her lips moist, parted slightly. The cold had turned her cheeks pink and snowflakes still dusted her auburn hair. Her lashes fluttered, but before she could look at him, he brought his mouth down on hers again. A soft sigh escaped her lips and she wriggled beneath him, arching up against him.

In all of his life, he'd never met a woman he couldn't charm—until Perrie Kincaid. Clever compliments and boyish grins just didn't work on her. She preferred the direct approach, like a spontaneous kiss in the snow—a kiss that was growing more passionate as time passed.

He tried to refocus on the feel of her mouth against his, but strange thoughts pressed at his mind. Why was he so attracted to her? He'd always preferred women who were sweet and biddable, not sharp-tongued and prickly. More likely, the challenge was in simply trying to get the upper hand with Perrie in their ongoing battle of wills. She was the last woman he should involve himself with...the last woman he should want.

Perrie must have read his mind, for at that moment, she pulled back and looked up into his eyes, her brow furrowed in confusion. Slowly she regained her sense of reality and her gaze cleared. She cursed softly, then pushed him off her. "What do you think you're doing?" she demanded.

Joe braced his hands behind him. "The same thing you were doing."

"Well, stop it!" Perrie brushed the snow off her jeans and jacket, then jumped to her feet.

"Are you sure you want me to stop?" Joe asked.

"I certainly don't want you kissing me anymore!"

Joe leaned back on his elbows and grinned at her. It wasn't hard to see that the kiss affected her as much as it did him. "Why? Afraid you were enjoying it?"

With a growl of frustration, she snatched up a handful of snow and threw it at his face, then turned on her heel and headed to the front steps of her cabin. "I didn't enjoy it. How could I enjoy it? I'd rather...stick my tongue on a frozen doorknob than kiss you again."

Joe stood up and brushed the snow from his clothes.

"Well, Kincaid, I'm sure you and the doorknob would have plenty in common."

She narrowed her eyes and glared at him, her gaze colder than the snow creeping down the back of his jacket. "Just stay away from me."

"You'll never win the competition. You're a city girl, Kincaid. You can't handle the wilderness. You're not cut out for it."

"What? You don't think I'm tough enough? Hey, I took a bullet in the arm to get a story. I'm a lot tougher than you think."

"All right," Joe conceded. "Though I consider a bullet in the arm for some damn newspaper article more stupid than tough."

"I'll win, if only to prove to you that I can."

"And if you do by chance win, I'll let you go to Cooper."

She braced her hands on her waist and kicked snow at him. "You'll *let* me go to Cooper?"

"Hey, I'm responsible for your safety, Kincaid. And I take my responsibilities seriously. But if you win, you can go to Cooper. I won't stand in your way."

"Damn right you won't stand in my way. I'll run right over you, Brennan. My footprints will be all over your chest."

Joe laughed. "Are you threatening me, Kincaid?"

"Just stay out of my way," she warned. She turned and hustled up the porch steps, but tripped along the way. With a vivid curse, she clambered to her feet and finally made it inside, slamming the door to punctuate her anger.

Joe sat in the snow for a long time, chuckling and shaking his head. If there was one thing he liked about Perrie Kincaid, it was that she always managed to surprise him. He'd never met a woman who could kiss him like a wanton one minute, then threaten to do him grave bodily harm the next.

PERRIE LAY IN BED, staring at the ceiling. Afraid to move, almost afraid to breathe, she clenched her teeth and prepared to push herself up. This was all Joe's fault. If it wasn't for his taunting the day before, she wouldn't have spent three hours yesterday working on her wood splitting.

She had tumbled into bed at sundown, crawling under the quilts to warm herself. Burdy arrived an hour later to take her to supper, but she could only call to him. Now, after a good night's sleep, she expected to feel refreshed. Instead, she felt as if she'd been run over by a cement truck, then rolled around in the hopper for good measure. If she hadn't been able to see her arms in front of her, she would have sworn they'd been pulled from their sockets and tied in a bow behind her back.

"Up," she muttered to herself. "Up, up, up."

Gritting her teeth, she rolled over and managed to rise to a sitting position, the pain streaking through her limbs. A hot bath would do much to relieve her aches and pains, but she wasn't sure she had the energy to drag the tub inside and fill it.

Her feet hit the cold floor just as a knock sounded on the front door. Wincing, Perrie stood up. Maybe she could sweet-talk Burdy into filling the bathtub for her. The crazy old guy seemed intent on making her stay as comfortable as possible. "Hang on, Burdy. I'm coming."

But Burdy McCormack wasn't the only one waiting on the other side of the door. A stranger stood on the porch, his long dark hair fluttering in the wind. She suspected the man that watched her with an indifferent expression was the notorious Hawk.

"Joe tells us you're goin' to enter the Muleshoe Games," Burdy said, hopping from foot to foot excitedly. "And then you're goin' to write about it in yer paper."

She winced, then rubbed her forearms. "I thought I'd give the games a try," she said, surprised by Burdy's interest. "As long as I'm stuck here. Besides, it would be a good angle for the story."

Burdy held out a folded sweatshirt and a cap, both with the Bachelor Creek Lodge logo emblazoned on them. "Well, you got yourself a sponsor, Miss Kincaid. Me and Hawk are goin' to train you, get you ready for the games."

Perrie smiled and shook her head. "I don't think Joe would approve."

"Well, we won't tell him, then," Burdy said. "Besides, I think it would be good publicity for the lodge. It's not every day we can git our names in a big city paper. We will git our names in the paper, won't we?"

Perrie contemplated Burdy's offer for a long moment. Though she could practice wood splitting and snowshoeing on her own, she had serious doubts that she'd be able to hop on a dogsled the day of the games and win the race. "If you and Hawk help me train, then I guess I could mention the lodge and my trainers as many times as I can in my article."

Burdy's head bobbed up and down and he laughed, the sound like a cackling chicken. "That's a deal, then. You git yerself dressed and meet us at the dog pens. Hawk is goin' to teach you how to mush."

Perrie wanted to beg off, to plead for a day's rest. But she had only one more week to train, and she couldn't pass up the opportunity to get behind the controls of a dogsled. Besides, Hawk did not seem like the type of man to tolerate any wimpy excuses about sore muscles and aching backs. "I'll be right out," Perrie said.

Hawk held up a pair of fur boots he'd been holding behind his back. "Mukluks," he said, as if that were all the explanation needed.

Perrie hesitantly reached out and took the gift from him. Stumbling around in the oversize boots Burdy had given her had been as exhausting as the wood splitting. And she suspected that it hadn't helped with her snowshoeing, either. "Thank you," she said softly, sending Hawk a grateful smile. "I really need these."

He didn't say more, just turned around and strode down the front steps. Burdy nodded, then ran after Hawk, leaving Perrie to wonder at their true motivations. Joe had made it clear that he didn't encourage her participation. But she had every right to enter the brides' competition—and every intention of winning first prize.

It was no small feat to get herself dressed, but she managed. As she tugged on the mukluks, she sighed in delight. Made of leather and fur, they were incredibly soft and warm and they fitted her feet perfectly. She imagined that her snowshoeing would improve immediately.

Fifteen minutes later, she found Burdy and Hawk at the dog pens. They stood near the sled, a simple invention made of bent wood tied with leather thongs. Burdy hustled toward her, then patted her on the shoulder. "You listen to Hawk, now. He'll teach you all you need to know."

"You're not staying?" Perrie asked.

"I got to go check my traplines," he replied.

"But, I—"

"Don't be scared of him," Burdy said in a quiet voice.

"He don't bite." With that, the old man hurried off, his cheery whistle breaking the still silence of the woods.

Perrie turned to Hawk and forced a smile. "So, where do we start?"

Hawk cocked his head and she followed him over to the dog pens. He opened the door, wading through the pack of jumping and barking dogs. "Come on," he ordered.

Gingerly, she stepped inside the pen. She'd never been a big fan of animals, especially in numbers greater than one. Her childhood hadn't included any pets except for a goldfish or two and an ant farm.

Hawk pointed to a huge white husky. "Loki," he said. "Lead dog."

"He's very...cute," Perrie commented, giving him a sideways glance. "So, how long have you known Joe Brennan?"

Hawk ignored her question. "Grab his collar and bring him to the sled."

Perrie's eyes widened. She could picture herself grabbing at the huge dog, only to have the husky eat her arm for lunch. The other dogs bumped and jostled her for attention, but Loki stood apart from the pack, watching her suspiciously. "Don't be a wimp," she murmured to herself.

Slowly, she approached, holding out her hand. "Hi, Loki," she said in a soft voice. "You're a pretty doggy. And a nice doggy, too. You're not going to—"

"Come, Loki!" Hawk's sharp command startled her and she jumped back as the dog moved toward her. But rather than attack her, the husky bounded to the door of the pen, and stood at Hawk's side.

Chagrined, Perrie followed the dog, then took his collar and led him out of the pen. She watched as Hawk demonstrated the process of putting on the dog's harness and hitching that harness to the towline. He pointed to the next dog, and this time, emboldened, she stepped inside the pen and grabbed the second husky.

"Come," she said firmly. The dog fell into step beside her and patiently allowed her to put him into the harness. She clipped him onto the towline and repeated the procedure over and over. Hawk watched her silently, allowing her to make her own mistakes. By the time the last dog had been harnessed, she felt confident in her abilities.

She brushed the snow off her jeans and straightened, waiting for Hawk to compliment her, but he stood silently, arms crossed over his chest. Perrie cleared her throat. "Why are you helping me with this?"

Again, she felt as if she were talking to a brick wall—a very handsome brick wall with penetrating gray eyes and a profile that had been sculpted by a master.

"Are you doing this to bust Brennan's chops?" Perrie asked. "Because if you are, I'm behind you one hundred percent."

Hawk bent down and showed her how to operate the snow hook, then guided her onto the runners of the sled. He stood behind her, their bodies nearly touching, his arms trapping her on the sled. She expected at least a minor reaction to his closeness. After all, he was an incredibly handsome man.

But she felt nothing, not even a tiny measure of what she experienced when Joe Brennan touched her. She bit back a silent curse. What was it about Brennan? Of all the men she'd known, he had the capacity to make her heart race and her breath disappear. And he also had the capacity to kindle her temper as no one had ever done before.

"Mush, Loki. Mush, boys. Hup, hup." The thirteen huskies darted forward until the towline snapped taut.

The sled jerked forward, and suddenly, they were skimming across the snow. Her thoughts of Joe forgotten, Perrie laughed out loud, holding tight to the sled for fear that she might fly off.

"Gee, Loki! Gee!"

The lead dog veered off to the left and she felt Hawk shift behind her, balancing the sled during the turn. She added her own weight to the turn, then smiled as the sled smoothly straightened and continued down the trail.

"Haw, Loki! Haw, boys!"

This time the sled turned to the right. Perrie cataloged the commands, carefully studying the way Hawk maneuvered the sled. They made their way down to the Yukon on a narrow trail and then circled back to the lodge. When Hawk called "Ho!" to the dogs, bringing them to a stop, she felt a sliver of disappointment.

He stepped off the back of the sled and Perrie moved to do the same, but he shook his head. "Try it on your own."

She blinked. "Really?"

He nodded.

Perrie drew a deep breath and pulled up the snow hook. "Mush!" she called. "Mush!" This time the dogs took off at an easy lope.

At first, Perrie was tentative, afraid to urge the dogs any faster. But after she'd called them through a series of curves in the trail, she shouted an enthusiastic "Hup, hup," and they responded with a burst of speed. Without Hawk's weight on the sled, it seemed to fly across the snow, and she had to take the turns very carefully to avoid losing control.

All around her, the woods were silent, only the squeaking of the sled runners and the shuffle of the dogs' paws to break the crystalline stillness. She completed the circuit from the river to the lodge three times, until Hawk waved her to a stop. Breathless, she hopped from the sled. "That was wonderful!" she cried. "I can't believe it was so easy."

"It isn't always easy. There are open creeks and fallen trees and moose that want to share the trail." Hawk moved to the front of the sled and began to unhitch the dogs.

Without a second thought, Perrie hurried to do the same. "I'm not sure that Brennan would approve of this," she ventured.

Hawk raised an eyebrow but didn't look at her. "Why is that?"

"Since I got to Muleshoe, Brennan has decided that I'm somehow too feebleminded to know what's good for me. He thinks he's protecting me by ordering me around. But he's driving me crazy."

"You confuse him," Hawk said.

Perrie opened her mouth to question his comment, but he turned away before she could speak.

"Now we feed the dogs," he said.

She trailed after him. "Wait a minute. What do you mean, I confuse him?"

"Just what I said." He handed her a pair of five-gallon buckets. "Go up to your cabin and fill these with water."

"*He* confuses *me*," Perrie said. "One minute he's yelling at me and the next he's throwing me down in the snow and—" She stopped short, aware of the flush of heat that slowly crept up her cold cheeks. "I—I just don't know what he wants from me. I can make my own decisions. If I want to return to Seattle, I should be able to—without asking his permission. Right?"

Hawk studied her for a long moment and she thought he might agree with her, or even explain the complexities of Brennan's behavior. "Water," he finally said, nodding to the buckets.

With a resigned sigh, Perrie trudged up to her cabin to fill the buckets. If Kyle Hawkins and Joe Brennan were such good buddies, just why was Hawk helping her?

Maybe he didn't approve of the way Joe was treating her, either. He seemed like a reasonable man, though it was hard to tell. He said only enough to get his point across and no more. But he was a good and patient teacher. The only thing she couldn't discern was whose side he was on.

One by one, she carried six buckets of water back to the dog pens. When she was finished, Hawk showed her how to mix the food for the dogs. In addition to regular dog food, she added bits of cooked moose liver and dried fish to the huge bowls, then stood outside the pens and watched as Loki and his pals greedily lapped up the feast.

"We'll train again tomorrow," Hawk said, staring down at the dogs.

"Why are you doing this?"

Hawk shrugged. "Nothing better to do," he said, turning to walk toward the lodge.

Perrie hurried after him, falling into step beside him, struggling to keep up with his long-legged stride. "If you really want to get to Brennan, you'd help me find a way to get back to Seattle. You must know another pilot who'd take me back. I'd be willing to pay you."

"Have the dogs hitched by noon," Hawk said, lengthening his steps until he was well ahead of her.

Perrie stopped and watched his retreat, cursing softly. It was clear Hawk was standing firmly on Joe Brennan's side. And he wasn't going to be any help at all in her quest to return to Seattle.

5

JOE PACED THE PORCH of the lodge, glancing through the woods at Perrie's cabin every few steps. He stopped and stared across the snow, then resumed his pacing.

"Just what are you up to, Kincaid?" he muttered.

If he hadn't known better, he'd have suspected she'd already achieved her escape from Muleshoe. Over the past few days, he'd barely caught sight of her. In fact, whenever he was around, she seemed to disappear. When Joe had asked Burdy what they'd been up to in the last few days, the old trapper had been oddly close-mouthed.

Whatever they'd been doing, it had kept Perrie out of his hair and off his case. He wasn't sure whether she was still training to enter the brides' competition in the Muleshoe Games. And to his knowledge, she hadn't made another attempt to engage a pilot. Perhaps she'd finally resigned herself to the fact that she'd be staying here in the wilderness until Milt Freeman said it was all right to go home.

The thought of Perrie leaving Muleshoe caused an unwelcome pang of regret. To be honest, he enjoyed her company. Even though they spent most of their time arguing, he found her to be a challenge. Unlike the other women he'd known, Perrie hadn't instantly fallen victim to his charms. He had a sneaking suspicion that turning on the charm did more to turn her off than anything else.

She was smart—not just intelligent, but clever, with a biting wit and the ability to see right through his motives. He liked sparring with her because she wasn't afraid to stand up to him. She kept him constantly off balance for he was never quite sure what she'd do or say to prove her point...and Perrie *always* proved her point.

He had found one chink in her armor, though. She liked to kiss him. And he sure as hell liked kissing her. His mind flashed back to the kiss they'd shared in the snow in front of her cabin, the feel of her body stretched beneath the length of his, the taste of her lips and the silken feel of her hair between his fingers.

If she hadn't put a stop to their roll in the snow, he wasn't sure where it would have led. All he knew was that Perrie Kincaid had a way of testing the limits of his control. Had she wanted, she could have teased him right into dragging her into her cabin and making love to her.

But she hadn't wanted. She'd taken him far enough to prove who was really in control and then she'd slammed on the brakes. But had it all been a game with her? Or had she experienced the same reckless desire that he had? There was something in the way she kissed him...

Normally, he maintained such rigid control around women, taking care to keep his emotions in check. But whenever he came within ten feet of Perrie, it was as if his oil pressure suddenly dropped and he lost all altitude. No matter what he did to compensate, he couldn't seem to keep himself level with the horizon.

If he didn't know better, he might think he was falling in love with her. But then, how the hell would he know? He'd never been in love before. And he wasn't sure that he'd even know love if it kicked him in the behind. Still, he knew what love *wasn't* and it wasn't supposed to be easy.

That was the problem. In all his relationships with women, everything had always been so easy. From the time he was old enough to notice the opposite sex, they were noticing him with undisguised appreciation. He'd cultivated his talent for charming women quite early in life and it had served him well. But it always seemed so simple...too simple. And anything that easy wasn't worth having, was it?

No, the only things worth having were the things he'd had to fight for, the things that offered up a challenge. Joe had never backed away from a challenge in his life. Hell, that's how he'd ended up in Alaska, why he'd jumped at the chance to fly search and rescue, why he continued to find himself drawn toward Perrie Kincaid.

He looked up to find himself standing at the door of her cabin. Frowning, he glanced back at the lodge. He had stepped outside to retrieve his logbook from the front seat of the Blazer, but somehow he'd ended up here. Cursing softly, he turned around, but then an idea struck him and he decided to knock.

"Hawk?" she called, her voice muffled by the door.

Jealousy tweaked his temper. Since when had Hawk been visiting her cabin? He hadn't even known they'd met. Hawk hadn't mentioned it. Besides, what could the two of them possibly have in common? Perrie never stopped talking and Hawk never seemed to start.

"Burdy?" she called after he didn't answer.

"It's Joe," he finally said.

"What do you want?"

By the sound of her voice, Joe could tell he was the last person she wanted to see. She slowly opened the door and stood looking up at him, tugging her bulky cardigan more tightly around her as if it might offer some type of protection. Frigid air and a spindrift of snow swirled around her feet and he noticed that she'd found some new footwear, a pair of handmade mukluks.

"New boots?"

She looked down. "Hawk gave them to me," she said.

Another surge of jealousy rushed through him, but he bit back a defensive reply and forced a smile. "Then you met Hawk?" he asked.

"A few days ago. What do you want?"

He felt her impatience growing and he scrambled for a reason for his visit, certain she was about to slam the door in his face. "I was wondering if you'd like to take a little trip."

Joe cursed inwardly. That wasn't what he'd intended to say at all! What the hell was he doing, inviting her to accompany him on a supply flight? Jeez, they'd actually have to be in each other's company, trapped inside the plane, for at least a few hours.

Perrie studied him suspiciously, then frowned. "What kind of trip?"

"I'm flying up to Van Hatten Creek, about sixty or seventy miles northwest of here, to deliver supplies. And I thought you might like to come along. But you don't have to if you don't want to." He almost hoped she'd refuse. "I have to warn you that if you go along, you're going to have to promise that you won't sneak off and try to get yourself back to Fairbanks."

"Today?" she asked.

"No, next month," Joe said sarcastically. "What? You have other plans?"

He watched as she considered his invitation for a long moment. What possible alternative did she have? It wasn't as if there were that much to do in Muleshoe. Unless she and Hawk had plans...with each other. He fought back the last rush of jealousy he'd tolerate and forced another smile. He would have thought a trip out of Muleshoe would be too tempting to pass up. After all, wasn't that what she'd been angling for since she arrived?

"All right," she replied. "I guess I'll come along."

He didn't expect to feel happy about her reply, yet he did. In fact, he was looking forward to spending the day with Perrie. Perhaps they'd be able to forget the animosity that hung between them and institute a truce of sorts. Maybe then she wouldn't have to run to Hawk for companionship.

"And if you're thinking about sneaking back to Seattle, you might as well know that the nearest settlement to the Gebhardts' cabin is about thirty-five miles away over pretty rough terrain. And John Gebhardt doesn't own a plane. And there are no roads, either. So, you still want to go?"

"I'm not thinking about sneaking off," she snapped, her eyes narrowing in anger. "Why do I get the distinct impression that you don't trust me, Brennan?"

He grinned, breaking the tension between them. "Gee, Kincaid, no wonder you're such an ace reporter. Here I thought I was fooling you. Now, get your jacket and mittens. And put a few more layers of clothing on. We're leaving in five minutes. I'll wait in the truck."

He turned and strode down the front steps of the porch, leaving her to stare after him. He could almost read her thoughts. What was he up to? she was wondering. Joe Brennan wasn't the type to do something nice for Perrie Kincaid, especially since she'd been such a pain from the instant they'd met.

Perhaps he *was* hoping for a truce of sorts. But it

would have to be an uneasy truce to begin with. If she thought for an instant he was letting down his guard, she'd be sorely mistaken. He wasn't about to go soft on his promise to Milt Freeman.

By the time he'd pulled the Blazer out of the shed and turned it around, she had made her way up to the lodge. She hopped inside the truck and slammed the door, then turned to Joe. To his utter surprise, she smiled at him. Not a cool, calculating smile, but a sweet and genuine smile, a smile that warmed his blood and made him forget his resolve.

"Thanks," she murmured. "I was starting to go crazy inside that cabin."

Without a reply, Joe put the Blazer in gear and maneuvered it up the narrow drive to the main road. He felt her gaze on him many times during their drive into Muleshoe and out to the airstrip, but he kept his eyes fixed on the road.

When they arrived at the airstrip, he drove right up to the Super Cub, then turned off the ignition. He watched as she searched down the row of planes for the familiar Otter that she'd arrived in, before her gaze returned to the Polar Bear Air logo on the tail of the Cub. Apprehension colored her expression, and for a moment she almost looked afraid. The Super Cub was a small plane, with room for only two, maybe three passengers, but it was the best plane for bush flying because it was able to take off and land virtually anywhere—gravel bars, frozen rivers, even on the side of a mountain.

"Nice plane," she murmured.

"You'll like the Cub. It's a great little plane."

"I think *little* would be the operative word here. Why are the wings fluttering like that?"

"They're made out of cloth," Joe replied.

"Cloth," she repeated.

He hopped out of the truck and ran around to her side. For a moment, he thought she might lock herself inside the Blazer and refuse to get into the plane. Obviously, there was a limit to her stubborn pride and her constant need to best him. That limit was sitting next to the truck, the stiff wind fluttering the fabric wings, the passenger cabin no larger than a carnival ride.

"You'll love it, I promise. It's a bluebird day, Kincaid. A day perfect for flying."

Perrie bit her bottom lip, then forced a smile as he helped her out of the truck and into the cramped rear seat of the plane. He slipped into the pilot's spot in front of her, and in moments the engine burst to life, the propeller a spinning blur in front of them.

They bumped down the snow-covered airstrip, gaining speed, the plane shuddering and shaking until it felt as if it would fly apart at the seams. Then, in an instant, they were airborne and the Cub rose like a bird on the wind, almost silently, save for the soft whine of the engine. He heard Perrie slowly release the breath she held and then a small sigh escaped her lips.

He turned and looked over his shoulder at her. "Are you all right?"

Her eyes were wide as she peered out the window, then looked at him. "This is incredible," she cried. "It's not like we're in a plane. I feel like a bird, like I'm flying under my own power. It's...it's so exhilarating."

Joe smiled and banked sharply to the north. "It's the only way to see Alaska, Kincaid."

"I knew it was wild, but until you see it from the sky, you don't realize how desolate it all is. It's almost frightening."

"Makes you feel kind of small, doesn't it? As if all the problems in your life are pretty insignificant."

"Yes," she said softly. "It does."

They flew for a long time in silence, then Joe banked the plane to the right and pointed out the window. "That's Van Hatten Creek," he said. "And you can see the Gebhardts' cabin in the little clearing to the south. You'll like the Gebhardts."

"We're going to land?" Perrie asked.

"Yeah. Whenever I deliver supplies, I stop and have lunch with John and Ann and their kids. Stuck out in the bush like this, they enjoy the company. And Ann's a helluva cook."

"But where are we going to land?" Perrie asked.

Joe glanced back to see her worriedly looking out the window for a break in the thick wooded terrain. "Right down there," he said. "Between the cabin and the creek."

"What? There's not enough room to land a plane down there. I thought we were going to throw the supplies out the window. I didn't know we'd be risking our lives on this trip."

"Sweetheart, I could put this plane down on the roof of their cabin if I had a mind to. You just watch. Like a walk in the park."

"This is no time to prove a point, Brennan. Just put the plane down where you normally do. And try not to kill us in the process."

He glanced back to see her fumbling with her seat belt. "Don't you trust me, Kincaid?"

"Not as far as I can spit," she replied.

Joe chuckled, then banked the plane to the left and began a sharp descent over the treetops. He heard Perrie cry out in alarm as they dropped out of the sky, the skis almost skimming the spruce forest below. And then, a tiny screech as they touched down. And finally, a long moan that stopped as soon as the plane did.

He unbuckled his seat belt and twisted around, only to see the color gradually return to Perrie's pale face. "What'd I tell you, Kincaid. Like a walk in the park."

PERRIE STUMBLED OUT of the plane on wobbly knees, grateful there was solid ground beneath her feet. She couldn't believe how they'd simply dropped out of the sky onto a tiny patch of snow. The plane had barely touched the ground before it skidded to a stop just yards from a thick stand of spruce. She'd been told that Joe Brennan was a great pilot, and now she'd seen proof.

She took a few steps then stumbled. He reached out to steady her, his hands lingering on her waist for a long moment. And then, to her surprise, he stole a quick kiss, his lips touching hers, sweet and fleeting. "Are you all right?" he asked, cupping her cheek in his hand.

Perrie nodded, flustered by Joe's sudden show of affection. The kiss seemed so natural, so easy that she momentarily forgot that he took such pleasure in making her miserable. Kissing him made her feel just the opposite, all shivery and flushed at the same time. "I—I'm glad we're on the ground," she murmured.

When she finally regained her composure, she turned to see a family hurrying toward the plane, the two small children, dressed in hooded fur parkas and tiny mukluks, stumbling through the snow to get to Joe. Joe scooped them both up in his arms and twirled them around before setting them back down.

"Did you bring us a treat?" the smallest child cried.

"Don't I always bring you a treat, Carrie?"

The little girl nodded, then grabbed Joe by the hand to

lead him back to the plane. While he unloaded the supplies from the Cub, the parents of the two children approached Perrie. They were both dressed in larger versions of the fur parkas that their children wore.

"I'm Ann Gebhardt," the woman said, holding out her mittened hand. "And this is my husband, John. And those are our two kids. Carrie, who's four, and Jack, who's three. Welcome to our home."

Joe stepped up beside her, a wooden crate balanced under each arm. "Ann, John, this is Perrie Kincaid." He paused. "She's a...friend who's visiting from Seattle."

Though she should have found his description of her awkward, she actually had to smile. Did Joe really consider her a friend? She'd assumed he thought of her as a thorn in his side, a thorn he enjoyed kissing every now and then, but a thorn nonetheless. But maybe they were becoming friends. The notion wasn't that distasteful—especially if it meant they'd be kissing each other on a regular basis.

Ann slipped her arm through Perrie's and led her toward the cabin. "For once, Joe brought *me* a treat. I don't think I've had an adult conversation with another woman for two or three months."

Perrie looked at her, shocked by the revelation. "I can't believe that."

"The last time we left the cabin was at Thanksgiving to visit friends who live thirty miles from here in Woodchopper. The winters are always a little lonely. But once summer comes, we do some traveling."

They slowly climbed the front steps of the cabin. Perrie glanced back to look at Joe, but he just grinned and gave her a wave, then turned back to the two children, who had tumbled into the snow at his feet. "I'd like to hear more about your life here," Perrie said.

"What could you possibly find interesting about my life?"

She laughed. "I'm a reporter. I find everyone's life interesting." In truth, she couldn't help but admire a woman who chose to live in the midst of the wilderness, a woman who faced true challenges every day.

Ann opened the front door of the cabin and showed Perrie inside. The tiny home was snug and cozy, a cheery fire blazing on the hearth and the smell of fresh-baked bread thick in the air. "This is my life," Ann said, tugging off her parka and fur mittens and hanging them on a hook beside the door. "It's hard to believe I once lived in a co-op in Manhattan and worked at one of the city's largest brokerage houses."

"You left New York City to come here? That must have been quite a change."

Ann took Perrie's jacket and pulled out a chair at the table near the fire. A few moments later, she placed a steaming mug of coffee in front of her, then turned to tend a cast-iron pot hung over the fire. "I came up here on a vacation six summers ago, and when it came time to go home, I couldn't. I just couldn't bring myself to go back to the rat race, so I chucked it all and moved here. I had plenty of money saved, enough to live on for years. I worked a few odd jobs and then I met John. He was teaching botany at Columbia and was here for the summer on a grant to study plant life near the Arctic Circle. After a month, he asked if I would marry him, and then we decided to stay here in Alaska so he could continue his work. And here we are, with two kids, living in the bush and loving every minute of it."

As Perrie sipped her coffee, she learned more about the Gebhardt family's life in the wilderness. After only a half hour, she felt as though she and Ann had been friends for years. Perhaps that's what living so far from civilization did—it made instant friends of perfect strangers.

She admired the woman's tenacity and strength, her incredible ability to make do with whatever the land offered and to be completely satisfied with her life. Perrie had always considered herself quite resourceful, but compared to Ann Gebhardt, Perrie Kincaid was a soft and spoiled city girl who couldn't survive a week without telephones, grocery stores and electricity. Maybe Joe was right. Maybe she didn't have what it took to live in the Alaskan wilderness.

They continued to talk as Ann set the table, until John and Joe burst in the front door, the children scampering around their feet. Joe had brought the family three crates of supplies and a small box of books for John's research. The family approached the delivery as if it were Christmas, delighting in each item as it was unpacked from the crates.

Once everyone had shrugged out of their parkas, they all sat down to eat a hearty meal of caribou stew and bread, fresh and warm from the oven. For dessert, Ann served a dried-apple tart with thick cream she poured from a can. It was the best meal Perrie had ever eaten, tasty and satisfying, more so because she knew how much work had gone into every ingredient.

The conversation during dinner was lighthearted. The Gebhardts were interested in any bit of news from the civilized world, and Joe recounted everything that was happening in Muleshoe, including the latest on the mail-order brides and the upcoming Muleshoe Games. Time after time, their gazes met across the table and she made no attempt to look away.

Ann and John listened to his stories closely, laughing

at the silly asides that Joe added to each story, and Perrie found herself completely enamored of her companion. He was so warm and witty that he could melt the heart of even the most jaded listener.

When he finally ran out of news, he and John grabbed the two children and settled in front of the fire for a game of Chutes and Ladders. Ann brought Perrie another cup of coffee and sat down across from her.

"Well, I've told you everything you wanted to know about living in the bush. Now it's time to tell me all about you and Joe. It's so nice to see that he's finally found someone."

"Found someone?" Perrie paused, then smiled in embarrassment. "You think that Brennan and I are... Oh, no. We're just friends. I mean, we're not even friends. Most of the time we pretty much hate each other."

Ann laughed. "I can't believe that. The way he looks at you. And the way you look at him. It's obvious how you two feel about each other."

"I—we—I mean, we're really just friends. We barely know each other."

"He's smitten. I've known Joe Brennan for a long time, and in that time, he's known a lot of women. But I've never seen him look at anyone the way he looks at you."

"How many women?" Perrie asked, her curiosity finally getting the best of her. "Just a ballpark figure."

"Well, I dated him for a few months," Ann admitted. "Until I met John. But there was never really anything between us."

"You dated Joe?" Perrie said, her voice filled with disbelief. She shook her head. "Are there any women left in Alaska that he hasn't dated?"

"He's a real charmer, our Joe. But that doesn't matter, now that he's found you."

"He didn't find me," Perrie said. "I was sort of dropped on his doorstep. He doesn't even like me."

"Oh, he definitely likes you. He may not realize it yet," Ann said. "But he will. Just you wait and see."

"I'm not going to be around long enough for that. As soon as I can, I'm heading back to Seattle. Back to civilization."

"That's what I said every day of my vacation six years ago. But this place just grabbed hold of me and wouldn't let go. To think that I almost went to Paris for two weeks instead of coming here. Sometimes little decisions have the ability to change the entire course of our lives. It must have been destiny." The last was said with a wistful smile as she turned her gaze to the two children playing in front of the fireplace.

They continued to talk of inconsequential things, but Perrie's thoughts returned again and again to Ann's odd assessment of Joe. Perrie had seen nothing in his behavior to indicate that he cared in the least for her. Sure, he'd kissed her a few times. But to hear Ann tell it, Joe Brennan had probably kissed half the female population of Alaska.

No, there was definitely nothing going on between them. Perrie Kincaid was an expert at reading the motives of those around her and she'd picked up nothing from Joe Brennan except hostility and disdain, punctuated by a few crazy moments of intense passion.

A few minutes later, Joe returned to the table with his empty coffee mug. "I'm afraid it's time for us to go. Perrie and I have one more stop before we head back to Muleshoe."

"So soon?" Ann cried. "It seems like you just got here."

Perrie stood and Joe helped her into her jacket. When she was all bundled up against the cold, she gave Ann a hug, then stepped back. Suddenly, she realized that she'd probably never see this woman again, and after they'd become such instant friends. Ann would live her life in the bush and Perrie would return to Seattle.

She wasn't sure what to say. "Have a nice life" seemed so trite, and "See you soon" sounded like a lie. In the end, she simply said goodbye and walked out the front door to the plane, turning back once to see Ann waving at her from the porch.

Joe helped her back into the plane and she continued to stare at the family. "They're really living life, aren't they?" Perrie murmured as he took his place in the seat in front of her.

"Yes," Joe said, "they really are."

"She's very brave. I don't think I could ever live out here."

"I bet you could," Joe replied. "In fact, I think you could do pretty much anything you set your mind to, Perrie. You just have to have a good reason to do it."

"What would I do out here? I mean, there are no newspapers to write for, no politicians to expose, no readers who want to know the truth."

"You don't even know what you're capable of until you try."

Joe started the engine on the plane and Perrie girded herself for a white-knuckle takeoff. Maybe Joe was right. Maybe she'd been so occupied with her career in Seattle that she'd never even considered any other options.

But why should she? She loved her job. And she was perfectly satisfied with her personal life. What more could she possibly want? She had no answer for that question, but she sensed that somehow Ann Gebhardt, a woman who lived in the middle of nowhere and existed on nothing, had much more than Perrie would ever have.

PERRIE STARED OUT the window of the Super Cub as it skimmed over a vast, flat landscape—endless white from horizon to horizon. It looked so different from the mountains and forests that surrounded Muleshoe. She glanced at her watch and realized they'd been in the air nearly a half hour, easily enough time to get back to the airstrip at Muleshoe.

She sat up and tapped Joe on the shoulder. "Where are we?" she asked.

"That's the southern edge of the Yukon Flats below us," Joe replied. "We're not far from Fort Yukon and the Arctic Circle. I thought we'd take a little side trip. I have something special I want to show you."

"We're that far north?" Perrie asked. "What are we doing up here?"

Joe looked over his shoulder and smiled. "You'll see," he said.

A few moments later, Perrie felt the plane begin to descend. "What's wrong?" she asked, trying to keep the panic from her voice.

"Nothing. We're going to land."

She stared down at the desolate wilderness below. Unlike the small area they'd landed in at the Gebhardts', there were plenty of wide open spaces to put down here. But there wasn't a cabin in sight. "There's nothing down there."

"There's a lot here," Joe replied, peering out the window, searching for something in the snow below. "You just have to look a little more closely."

He finally set the plane down on a wide, treeless expanse of snow, landing so smoothly the only thing that told her she was on the ground was the hiss of snow beneath the plane's skis. He shut the engine down, then helped her out of the plane, tossing a pair of down sleeping bags at her feet.

"We're spending the night here?" Perrie asked.

He threw a thick blanket over the engine to keep it warm. "Only if you get really lucky," he teased. "Come on."

They walked away from the plane, his eyes scanning the area, still searching. Then he stopped and unrolled the two sleeping bags. Wrapping one around her shoulders, he pointed to the ground. Once she was settled, he sat down beside her in the snow and handed her a pair of binoculars.

"Are you going to tell me what we're looking for?"

"Just be quiet and watch," he said.

They sat, silently, for more than a half hour. Though the sun was bright and the air calm, she still felt the cold seeping into her bones. She was about to ask him when they would leave when he slowly raised his arm and pointed to the horizon. "There," he murmured.

She held up the binoculars and stared out over the snow. A movement in her field of vision caught her attention and she carefully focused. Her breath caught in her throat as a huge gray wolf appeared out of the snow.

"I saw him for the first time about three years ago," Joe explained. "I was flying some supplies up to Fort Yukon in the Otter and had some engine trouble, so I had to put the plane down. I was working on the engine when all of a sudden I looked up and there he was, watching me."

"Weren't you afraid?"

"Wolves aren't aggressive. They're afraid of man and would never attack unless they're provoked. Or sick. I think he was just a little lonely, wandering around out here on his own. He was a lone wolf, a male without a family. Probably kicked out of his pack by the alpha male."

Perrie glanced over at him. "Burdy called you a lone wolf once."

Joe smiled. "I guess I am. But not as alone as Romeo was. He was completely alone."

"Romeo?"

"That's what I named him. Every time I flew up here I'd check on him. Sometimes I wouldn't see him for months, and then, there he'd be. He's harder to spot in the winter since he has to wander farther for food. But I think he's starting to recognize the sound of my plane."

"Really?" Perrie asked.

Joe laughed. "No. I'd just like to think we're friends."

"You do have a lot in common."

"Maybe." He paused, scanning the area with his binoculars again. "At least we did, until he found Juliet. Look, there she is."

Perrie trained her binoculars to the left of Romeo. Standing near the huge gray wolf was a smaller black wolf. "His mate?"

"Yeah. Romeo finally decided to settle down a couple years back. I guess he got tired of playing the field."

"Maybe you should have given him some advice," Perrie teased. "The way I hear it, you've got quite a way with the ladies."

"Don't believe everything you hear," Joe said.

"If I were writing a story on your love life, Brennan, I'd have more than enough confirmation to go to print." Perrie studied the wolves for a long moment, then put the binoculars in her lap and looked at Joe. "What about you?" she asked. "Do you ever think about finding a Juliet?"

"Wolves mate for life. I'm not sure I'm the type to be with one woman forever."

"Me, neither," Perrie said. "I mean, with one man. I suppose some people are happy with that. But I've never met a man that I could imagine spending the rest of my life with."

"Maybe you just haven't met your Romeo," he said softly, looking down at her.

"And maybe you haven't met your Juliet," she countered.

His gaze locked with hers, and for a moment, she thought he might kiss her. But then he turned away. "Look," he said. "There's the rest of the family."

Three other wolves appeared behind Juliet, about the same size as their mother but lankier.

"They had five pups last summer," Joe explained, "but they lost two of them sometime in the fall. I'm not sure what happened."

"That's sad," she said.

"That's life in the wilderness," he replied. He glanced at her again. Then, without hesitation, he leaned over and touched his mouth to hers. His lips were incredibly warm, sending a pulse of heat through her body that seemed to drive away the cold.

His tongue teased at hers, and for an instant, she thought about drawing away. But her common sense had fled and she was left with only instinct and the overwhelming need to have more. Unlike their first, challenging kiss or the frantic meeting of mouths that they'd experienced in the snow, this kiss was different. It was slow and delicious, filled with a longing that she didn't know existed between them.

She didn't want him to stop this time. Instead, she wanted to pull him down on top of her and find out how Joe Brennan really felt about her. And how she felt about him. As if he read her thoughts, he gently pushed her back into the soft down sleeping bag, his lips never leaving hers.

Everything that had stood between them—the arguments, the mistrust, the fight for control—simply dissolved, swept away by the stark solitude of the wilderness. They were completely alone, a brilliant blue sky above and nothing but untamed country all around them.

She felt wild, primal, uninhibited, like the wolves they'd watched, driven by instinct and pure need. She wanted to touch him, to feel his skin beneath her fingertips, to run her hands through his hair. Impatiently, she slipped off her mittens then clutched at the front of his down jacket, pulling him closer.

He groaned softly, his breath hot against her mouth. "We're doing it again," he murmured. "You're making me crazy, Kincaid."

"I know," Perrie said, breathless. "We should stop. But I don't want to stop."

"No, we shouldn't stop," Joe said, tugging off his gloves. "Not this time." He pushed her hat off to furrow his hands into her hair. Tipping her head, he kissed her again, deeper and longer, his mouth plundering hers until her head spun with uncontrolled desire.

She shuddered, the passion radiating through her in waves. Joe pulled his sleeping bag over them both, creating a warm cocoon. Slowly, he tugged at the zipper of her jacket, then slipped his fingers beneath the layers of sweaters she wore. When he finally met warm skin, she heard him suck in his breath and hold it.

"This is not the place to do this," Joe said. "It's ten below zero."

"It's warm enough," Perrie said.

Joe pushed himself up, then looked at her, playfully running his finger along her bottom lip. "But there are much warmer places to be, sweetheart. We don't have to risk frostbite to be with each other."

Perrie closed her eyes. "You know, we'd be risking a lot more than frostbite if we let this happen again." Her common sense had returned in full force and she sat up and tugged her jacket closed. "This is ridiculous, Brennan. We can't keep doing this."

"Why not?" Joe asked.

Perrie opened her mouth to reply, then realized she didn't have a good reason. There had to be a reason. "Because we can't."

Joe nuzzled her neck. "That's not a good reason, Kincaid. If you ask me, we do it pretty well."

"That is not the point," she scolded, pushing him away.

"What is the point?"

"I don't know." The truth was, she *did* know, but she was too embarrassed to put her feelings into words. She liked Joe Brennan and she liked it when he kissed and touched her. And she thought about him a lot more than she wanted to. The problem was, she didn't want to be like all the other women who had lost their hearts to a quick smile and handsome face. "I—I don't know," she repeated softly.

"Well, until you do, I'm going to keep kissing you, whenever and wherever I want."

Perrie zipped her jacket then began to search for her mittens and her hat. "I think we'd better go now."

Joe grabbed her hand and pulled her back down. A long, lingering kiss shook her resolve and she found herself slipping back into the languid pool of desire she had just left behind.

"Whenever and wherever," Joe murmured, nibbling at her lower lip. With a teasing grin, he kissed the end of her cold nose, then scrambled to his feet. He offered her a hand up and she took it, expecting him to draw her back into his arms.

But he didn't. Instead, he grabbed the sleeping bags from the ground and tucked them beneath his arm. "Come on, Kincaid. Let's get you back home where you'll be warm and safe."

6

THE STORY SEEMED to tumble out of her head, word after word, sentence after sentence, as if the entire text had been there all along. The wolves and the Gebhardts, two families living in the midst of the wilderness, bent on survival. Perrie had stayed up all night putting her thoughts onto paper, rewriting each phrase until it was as perfect as it could possibly be.

She wasn't sure what had made her pick up pencil and paper. She had barely stepped inside the door of her cabin after saying a quick and uneasy goodbye to Joe, before she sat down and began to write. And until she began, she hadn't realized that her day with Joe had affected her so deeply.

Joe had called her name as she ran back to the cabin, but she'd been intent on putting some distance between them. Whenever they were together, all her resolve went right down the drain. Either they fought like a pair of pit bulls or they jumped on each other like a couple of hormone-charged teenagers. Until she figured out exactly how she wanted to handle Joe Brennan, she was going to stay away from him. So she wrote.

The day had faded, and rather than switch on a light, she brought an old kerosene lamp to the table. The soft glow seemed to enfold her in a world of her own making, a world without modern conveniences...deadlines and sources...story meetings and proofreaders. For the first time in many years, she wrote from her heart, not from her head. And she rediscovered the true joy of crafting a beautiful sentence, of taking a reader to a place they'd never been.

She had worked all night, catching only snatches of sleep before another turn of phrase would invade her dreams and she'd need to get up and jot it down. Then she would sleep again, and sometimes, mingled with the images of the wolves, she'd see Joe and he would become part of her story, personifying the wolf who had roamed the frigid winters alone.

She had tried to put their encounter in the wilderness out of her head. But it returned again and again. At first, throwing herself back into her work had been an antidote, the perfect way to put his kisses out of her head. But later, she enjoyed the memories, lingering over them as she wrote, reliving the feel of his hands on her body, his mouth over hers.

The day had dawned bright and clear, and when Perrie awoke she saw the story scattered beside her over the quilt. Slowly, she reread what she'd written, making a few more edits. Then she got up and carefully recopied the text onto clean paper. Though she'd brought her laptop along with her, this story didn't want to be written on a computer. This story was more like a letter—a letter from the wilderness.

Although this wasn't the type of story she usually wrote, she was still proud of how it came out. And she was anxious to find out if Milt thought there was any merit in the writing. Not that he'd run the story, but perhaps he'd enjoy her insights on Alaska.

"A fax machine," she murmured, tugging a bulky knit sweater over her head. "They've got to have a fax machine up at the lodge." Perrie retrieved her mukluks from near the door and pulled them on, then grabbed her jacket and the sheaf of paper that was her story.

The air was crisp and biting and her breath clouded in front of her face as she trudged up to the lodge. The low log building had stirred her curiosity more than once since she'd arrived, but she'd tried to avoid it, knowing that Joe lived inside. She preferred the privacy of her own cabin.

As she stepped up onto the wide porch, she noticed an old carving above the door. No Wimin Kin Pass. Perrie smiled. Obviously the bachelors who lived inside felt it necessary to protect themselves from predatory females. Below the large block letters, she read another phrase. "Except for Julia," she murmured.

Perrie stepped back, wondering who Julia was and why she was admitted entrance to the lodge. "Well, if Julia can go inside, I certainly can," Perrie said.

She hesitated for a moment and tried to come up with an offhand greeting for Joe. After what had passed between them yesterday, she wanted to make it clear that she would not tolerate any more spontaneous kissing...or touching. She'd be polite and friendly. And when she felt that familiar surge of desire that raced through her whenever he came near...well then, she'd just turn around and walk away.

Her resolve firmly in place, Perrie rapped on the front door and waited for a reply. But when no one came to answer, she knocked again. After the third try, she decided to venture inside.

The interior of the lodge was a complete surprise. She expected something as rough as the exterior. But instead, she entered a huge room that combined a cozy country feel with rugged log walls and a stone fireplace. Brightly colored woven blankets draped the chairs and sofa, and scattered about the room were interesting little pieces of Alaskan art—a carving here, a handwoven basket there. Rag rugs covered the plank floors and a fire snapped and popped in the fireplace. Compared to her bare-bones cabin, the lodge was backwoods luxury.

"Hello?" she called. "Is anybody home?"

Her call was answered by a high-pitched voice and a flurry of footsteps. A small boy, pale-haired and wide-eyed, appeared from the rear of the other side of the great room. "I'm here!" he cried.

When he saw her, he stopped short then adjusted his glasses on his upturned nose. "Who are you?" he asked.

"I'm Perrie. Who are you?"

"I'm Sam. I live here. Are you looking for my dad?"

Perrie frowned. "That depends on who your dad is," she said. Joe hadn't said a word about having a son, and Hawk didn't seem like the fatherly type. One of the brides had mentioned that the third partner in the lodge had recently married, but he hadn't been married long enough to have a child so old. "I'm looking for Joe."

Sam sauntered up to her side and studied her unabashedly. "Joe isn't my dad, he's my uncle. Well, he's not really my uncle, he's more like a big brother. Or maybe my best friend. My dad's name is Tanner. He's really my stepdad. We flew in from Fairbanks this morning." His eyes twinkled. "Boy, are my arms tired." A giggle burst from his lips and Perrie couldn't help but smile. His laughter was infectious. "That's a joke," he said.

"I know," Perrie replied, joining in his delight.

"What is going on in here?" A slender blonde appeared next to Sam, a dish towel clutched in her hands. "I can hear you all the way in the kitchen!" She stopped when she saw Perrie, then regarded her with a curious gaze.

"I'm sorry," Perrie said. "I knocked, but there was no answer. I'm looking for Joe."

A smile touched the woman's lips. "Are you Joe's Perrie?"

Perrie returned her smile hesitantly. "No. I mean, yes. I'm Perrie...but I'm not..." Her words trailed off. Trying to explain exactly what she was to Joe Brennan was becoming more complicated every day.

"I was just going to walk up to your cabin and meet you!" the woman cried. "I'm Julia Lo—I mean, Julia O'Neill. I've only been married a month. It's strange getting used to the new name." She paused. "So, how has your stay been? Have you been comfortable? I hope Joe has been taking good care of you. He's not usually in charge of hospitality, but Tanner and I have been at loose ends this last month, with the wedding and the move and—" Julia paused again. "Would you care for some breakfast? I've made some muffins."

"Is Joe here?" Perrie asked.

"He's down at the airstrip with my husband. They're unloading all our things. Sam and I just closed up our apartment in Chicago. We're going to be living here now. Is there something I can help you with?"

"I was wondering if the lodge has a fax machine," Perrie asked.

"We sure do. Tanner just put one in last month. It really helps with the reservations and trip details. It's in the kitchen." Julia motioned Perrie to follow her and they walked through a large dining room filled with old tables and a hodgepodge of antique and handmade chairs. Beyond a swinging door was a huge kitchen, as rustic and cozy as the rest of the lodge.

"The fax machine is over there by the phone," Julia said. "Why don't you send your papers and then we'll sit down and visit?"

Like Ann, Julia seemed anxious for female company. Perrie suspected that adjusting to life in Muleshoe was difficult, especially coming from a city like Chicago. Yet Julia seemed incredibly happy and excited, the same as Ann had been. They had their husbands and their families and a life full of challenges.

Perrie had her job. That had always been enough, more challenge than she could handle at times. But when compared to carving out a life in Alaska, Perrie's twenty-four-hour-a-day job as an investigative reporter seemed to lose a bit of its luster.

Sure, people in Seattle knew her name and they waited to read her stories. And she waited, impatiently, for someone to do something wrong. That summed up her whole career. She preyed on the indiscretions of others, exposing their foibles to the entire city of Seattle and delighting in their punishment. Without criminal intent and old-fashioned greed, she wouldn't have a job.

When she looked at it like that, she suddenly saw her career unfold in front of her. What would she be doing in a year...five years...ten years? Would she still be watching and waiting, hoping that some prominent person might take a step on the wrong side of the law? Would she still eat, breathe and sleep her work? Or would she find a new road to take, the way Ann and Julia had?

"Perrie? Do you know how to operate this machine?"

Startled from her musings, Perrie turned and nodded to Julia. "Yes. I—I was just trying to remember the number."

Page by page, her story went through the phone lines

from Muleshoe, Alaska, all the way to Seattle. Within a few hours, Milt would read it. She could already hear his tirade as he wondered where her brides story was. In another few days, she'd take part in the Muleshoe Games and she'd finish the story she'd been assigned. And then she'd go home to her comfortable apartment and her exciting career.

"Would you like to sit down and have a cup of coffee?" Julia asked.

Perrie stared down as the last pages slipped into the machine. "I—I can't. I really have some things to take care of." The truth be told, now that she'd avoided Joe's company, she wanted to get out of the lodge before he returned. She wasn't at all sure that she had enough resolve to keep from wanting him as much as she had the last time they were together.

"I can't believe you're comfortable up at that cabin," Julia said. "We have an extra room here in the lodge. You're welcome to stay down here."

"My cabin is fine," Perrie replied.

"But traipsing to the outhouse and hauling in that tub to take a bath..."

"It's all part of the wilderness experience."

"Well, I certainly couldn't put up with it," Julia said.

Perrie frowned. "But you live here."

"And we have a bathroom," Julia said.

A gasp broke from Perrie's throat. "A bathroom? An indoor bathroom? You don't have to walk to the outhouse in the middle of the night?"

"Of course not," Julia said. "That's why I couldn't understand why you'd choose to live in one of the cabins when you could have stayed down here."

"I could have stayed here in the lodge?"

"I did when I first came here," Julia said. "Although

I'm not surprised that Joe put you out in one of the cabins, considering the legend."

"What legend?"

"There's a carving above the door. The prospectors that lived here during the gold rush believed that any woman who crossed the threshold of the lodge would marry one of the inhabitants."

"And I've been hiking to the outhouse in subzero weather and bathing in the sink because Joe Brennan thinks I might decide I want to marry him?"

Julia considered Perrie's words for a moment, then nodded as if the logic were quite acceptable. "Yes, I suppose so."

"Julia, where do you want these boxes?" The sound of Joe's voice echoed through the lodge and Perrie's temper bubbled. The kitchen door swung open and he stood in the doorway, boxes piled so high they blocked his face.

"You can put them down here," Julia said, glancing nervously between Perrie and Joe.

Joe lowered the stack to the floor, then straightened, coming face-to-face with Perrie. He blinked in surprise, then gave her an uneasy smile. "'Morning," he murmured. She expected to be uncomfortable with him, especially after what they'd shared the day before. But she'd also thought they'd left all the anger behind them, that they'd become friends. She'd been sadly mistaken.

"You put Perrie out in a cabin?" Julia asked. "Without heat and indoor plumbing? You made her cook her own meals and make her own bed? Is this any way to treat a guest here?"

Joe scowled at Julia. "She's not really a guest."

"Aren't we being paid by her newspaper? Isn't it true that our rate includes all meals?"

"Well, yes. But this is a different situation."

Julia slowly approached Joe until they stood toe to toe. "Here's the situation. I want you to go up to Miss Kincaid's cabin, gather her belongings and bring them back here to the lodge. And then I want you to make our guest as comfortable as possible."

Perrie stiffened her spine and forced a smile. "That's really not necessary. I'm perfectly happy staying in the cabin." With that, she sent Joe a murderous look—a look that said there would be no more long, deep kisses between them. And the last thing she wanted to do was sleep under the same roof as Joe Brennan.

She stalked out of the room, cursing softly with each step. Her thoughts, a jumble of anger and frustration, detoured to an image of Joe Brennan, naked, asleep amid rumpled sheets...finely muscled chest...long, sinewy arms.

"Stop it," she scolded out loud. "You should be thinking about how you're going to get back to Seattle, not wondering what Joe Brennan looks like in bed."

JOE WATCHED as Perrie stormed out of the kitchen. He shook his head and wagged his finger at Julia. "You enjoy making me squirm, don't you?"

Julia grinned, then stepped over to him and gave him a kiss on the cheek. "I'm going to turn you into a sensitive male if it takes me the rest of my life."

Joe growled. "I should have known you women would stick together."

"There are precious few of us here at the lodge, Brennan," Julia said, wiping her lipstick from Joe's cheek. "I'll do everything I can to even the odds a bit."

Joe picked up a box and hefted it onto the counter. "Don't even think about it. Just because Perrie Kincaid stepped over that threshold does not mean I'm going to marry her. We don't even like each other."

That wasn't entirely true, Joe thought to himself. He liked Perrie more than he wanted to admit. But right now, he would venture that she didn't have a particularly high opinion of him.

"She seems like a lovely woman," Julia said. "I already like her."

Hawk and Tanner strode into the kitchen at that very moment, with Sam hard on their heels. "Hey, I just saw Perrie Kincaid on the porch," Tanner said. "Did she come inside?"

Joe cursed and sent Tanner a poisonous glare. "Don't you start with me. Your wife has already covered that subject quite thoroughly. No, I won't be marrying Perrie Kincaid. Hell, if she's going to marry anyone here, it will be Hawk. She can't seem to stop talking about him." Just the thought brought a nagging jealousy, but it was about time Joe found out what really was going on between the two of them.

Tanner and Julia both turned an inquisitive gaze in Hawk's direction. "Well," Julia said, "what do you have to say for yourself?"

"I gave her mukluks," Hawk replied. "I'm helping her get ready for the Muleshoe Games."

Joe's jaw dropped. "You're helping her?"

Hawk nodded.

"Do you know why she wants to win the brides' competition? So she can get herself up to Cooper and find a pilot to fly her back to Seattle, where someone will probably take another shot at her. She's here in Muleshoe for her own safety."

"You sound awfully concerned for the lady," Tanner commented.

"For a lady he doesn't even like," Julia added as she wandered over to the fax machine. "Perrie left her papers here. Why don't you take them up to the cabin? And while you're there, you can apologize for your inhospitable attitude. Invite her to have dinner with us. And tell her she can stay in the spare room."

"I wouldn't have to apologize if you hadn't made her mad," Joe said, snatching the sheaf of papers from Julia's hand.

"Just kiss her," Sam suggested. "That's what Tanner does when my mom gets mad."

Joe ruffled Sam's hair as he passed. "I'll keep that in mind. I daresay I trust your advice a whole lot more than I trust your mom's."

He made the trip up to Perrie's cabin slowly, not because he loathed the thought of apologizing to her, but because as he walked, he read the story that she'd left behind. With every step, he was drawn more deeply into her words, the stunning visual images she created out of a simple turn of phrase. He'd always known she was a writer, but he never expected she possessed such talent. He thought she wrote about criminals and politicians and greedy businessmen. Not about wolves and the wilderness and the bonds of family.

He finished her story as he stood on the front porch of her cabin, and when he read the last word, he sat down on the top step and read it all over again. He sat there a long time, thinking about Perrie and the wolves, about loneliness and love. And he realized that he had been wasting his time.

Sooner or later, Perrie Kincaid would go back to Seattle and she'd be gone from his life for good. There was a time when he had wished for that day. But now, he wanted her to stay. Something had drawn them together yesterday at the Flats and he needed to know what it was—because it wasn't just simple lust.

He wanted Perrie Kincaid more than he'd ever wanted a woman before. But he didn't want her in his bed—at least that wasn't the only place he wanted her. He wanted her beside him when he watched the wolves the next time, and he wanted her across the breakfast table tomorrow morning. He wanted to show her the northern lights and the beauty of an Alaskan summer. He wanted her to be there when the ice broke on the Yukon and when it froze again in the winter.

Most of all, he wanted time. Time to figure out why he wanted more time. Time to find out if this fascination he had with her was transitory, or whether he'd be cursed with it for the rest of his life. Time to come to the conclusion that he and Perrie Kincaid weren't meant to fall in love and get married.

The door behind him opened and he turned to find Perrie watching him. Her arms were crossed over her chest and she still looked angry. "How long are you going to sit out here?"

He held up the story. "You left this at the lodge."

She took it from him and rolled it up. "I'm not moving to the lodge."

"I didn't expect you would." He paused. "It's a wonderful story, Kincaid. As I was reading it, I could see it all over again. You have an incredible talent. Why do you waste it writing about criminals?"

She walked to the porch rail and looked out at a stand of spruce. "What I do is important," she said evenly. "It makes a difference. This is a silly story about wolves. It doesn't make a difference to anyone."

"It makes a difference to me, Perrie. It makes me feel something inside. When I read it, it moved me."

Perrie turned and stared at him blankly, as if she didn't understand what he was trying to say, then shook her head. "It's nothing," she said firmly, folding the papers up and shoving them in the back pocket of her jeans. She took a deep breath and pushed away from the porch railing. "Where's Burdy?"

"He's probably in his cabin."

"I need some breakfast. I want to go into Muleshoe."

Joe stood up and moved toward her. "I could take you," he offered. When she backed away, he stopped and held up his hand.

"I'd rather go with Burdy," she said.

"Listen, I know you're angry. And I'm sorry. I should have asked you to stay in the lodge. It's much more comfortable and—"

"It doesn't make a difference," Perrie replied in a cool voice. "I wouldn't have stayed there anyway. The cabin is just fine."

"No, it's not. It's—"

"What do you want from me?" she snapped. "Do you need absolution for being a jerk? Do you think complimenting my writing is going to smooth everything out?"

"I thought that—"

"I don't belong here," she said in a weary voice. "I belong back in Seattle. And you're the one who's keeping me here."

"I know how important your work is to you, but I made a promise to Milt and I'm going to keep it."

"A promise to make me miserable?"

"A promise to keep you safe."

"But why you?"

Joe had never told another soul what Milt Freeman had done for him. But now it was time to tell Perrie.

Maybe then she'd understand why it was so important for her to stay in Muleshoe.

"Right after I got out of law school, I worked for the public defender's office in Seattle. I was so full of myself, thinking I'd stand up for the rights of the common man and make the world a better place. But that wasn't the way it turned out. Mostly, I represented criminals. But I did my job very well.

"One day, I had the pleasure of representing a young punk named Tony Riordan. He was your basic wise-guy wannabe who'd been running a small extortion business shaking down some of Seattle's immigrant shopkeepers. I represented him, I lost the case, and he went to jail for six months."

Perrie's jaw dropped. "You knew Tony Riordan?"

"Intimately. After the trial, Mr. Riordan took it upon himself to send a few of his associates to my house to express his displeasure at the verdict. But before I got home that day, a reporter named Milt Freeman called me and warned me. He'd heard from one of his sources that Tony wanted a little payback."

"So Milt saved your life?"

"Or at least my pretty profile," Joe said with a laugh. "The point is, Tony Riordan was dangerous back then and he had nothing to lose. He's got a lot more to lose now, Perrie, and you're the one who's threatening to take it away."

"I can take care of myself," Perrie said stubbornly, crossing her arms over her chest.

Joe cursed softly. "Is it so hard to believe that someone cares about you?" Her mouth tensed into a thin line and Joe knew that he'd finally driven his point home. "Milt cares about you. And I care about you."

A cynical smile curled her lips and her chin tipped up

defiantly. "I guess you'll do anything to keep me here, won't you." She started down the front steps. "I've got to find Burdy."

"Come on, Perrie," he chided, following after her. "You can't stay mad at me forever."

She turned, grinning at him as she swaggered backward. "Just watch me, Brennan."

"Why can't you think of this as a learning experience?" he called. "I bet you'll never walk into your bathroom again without appreciating the beauty of indoor plumbing. Or turn up the heat without remembering the wood you hauled to feed the stove in the cabin."

"Keep talking, Brennan. Sooner or later you might just convince yourself that you're doing a good thing by keeping me here."

He stopped and watched her walk toward Burdy's, admiring the quick sway of her hips, the focused energy of her stride. Chuckling to himself, he started back toward the lodge.

It was getting harder and harder to stay angry at Perrie Kincaid. To tell the truth, the more he knew of her, the more he liked her. She was stubborn and opinionated and she knew her own mind. She didn't let anybody push her around. He admired that about her.

Beyond that, he thought she was just about the prettiest woman he'd ever known. He'd never really looked at her as anything but a pain in the backside, tough as nails and prickly as a hawthorn tree. But then, out of the clear blue, he had come to realize just how incredibly alluring she was.

Joe shook his head. That was one opinion he'd have to keep to himself. It wouldn't do to have everyone in the lodge and all of Muleshoe know that he was attracted to Perrie Kincaid.

PERRIE SLID ONTO a bar stool and grabbed a menu. Paddy Doyle lumbered over and wiped his hands on his apron. "Miz Kincaid. How are you this sunny morning?"

"I'm fine, Mr. Doyle. I think I'll have a lumberjack breakfast...with an extra order of bacon...cheese on the hash browns...and a double milk."

Paddy raised his eyebrow. "You sure you want all that for breakfast? You usually just have a doughnut and coffee."

"I'm in training," Perrie said.

Paddy scribbled her order on a scrap of paper, then walked it back to the kitchen. He returned a few moments later with a large glass of milk. "I heard you're entering the brides' competition," he said. "All the bachelors around town are lookin' forward to seeing how you fare. See if you're decent marriage material."

Perrie smiled. "The rules say any single woman can enter. But this single woman isn't interested in marriage. Just in the first prize."

"I also heard that you spent some time inside the Bachelor Creek Lodge this morning."

Perrie blinked in surprise. She'd visited the lodge less than an hour ago and already Muleshoe's version of Walter Cronkite was on the story. "My first and last visit."

"I wouldn't be too certain of that. A lady sets foot in the lodge and she's bound to be married." Paddy laughed. "Not one of them boys paid a cent into the bride scheme and now they're falling like tall timber. First Tanner. Now Joe. Hawk will be next."

"I'm not marrying Joe Brennan," Perrie insisted.

"I bet Joe was plenty mad when he found out you got inside the lodge. He's been dodging marriage since I met him five years ago. You know, he's dated pretty near every available woman in east Alaska."

"I know that, Mr. Doyle. Everyone knows that. Seems Joe's social life is front-page news around Muleshoe."

"Would be, if we had a newspaper." Paddy rubbed his chin. Bracing his foot on an empty beer barrel, he leaned up against the bar. "You work in the newspaper business, right?"

"When I'm not withering away in the wilds of Alaska," she said, sipping at her milk.

"I need some advice." Paddy reached back and untied his apron. "Come with me. I want to show you something."

Her curiosity piqued, she followed him through the bar to a rear door, then up a dusty narrow stairway to the second story of the building. Paddy came to another door and threw it open.

"This stuff has been up here forever," he said. "I was thinkin' about putting in a nice dance hall up here, for parties and weddings and such."

"What is this?" Perrie asked.

"This is what's left of the *Muleshoe Monitor*," Paddy explained. "Paper started when this was a boomtown during the gold rush days. Lasted until the thirties and then the old guy that ran it moved to Fairbanks."

"This is incredible," Perrie said, moving to stand near the line of old wood cabinets on the wall. The galleys from the final edition of the *Monitor* still lay on the table, covered with years and years of dust. She brushed off the masthead to get a better look. "When I was in junior high, I worked for my town newspaper. They had all the old block type left and they used it for signs and posters. I would sit and cast headlines. Local Girl Wins Pulitzer,

Kincaid Awarded Nobel Peace Prize. Things like that. Now it's all done on computer."

"I want to sell this stuff," Paddy said. "What do you think it's worth?"

Perrie picked up a composing stick. "This is...probably not worth much. I'm not really sure. To someone like me, it's fascinating. When I was a kid, I dreamed about having my own paper."

"Back when Muleshoe was a boomtown, in '98, we had enough folks living here to support a paper. Nearly two thousand. And with all the money bein' made, there was plenty of news. The guy that ran the place passed on in 1951 and no one ever came back to claim his property. That press has been sittin' there ever since, collecting dust. Probably take half the men in this town to move the thing. Or I guess we could break it apart."

"Oh, no!" Perrie cried. "You can't do that."

Paddy shrugged. "Not much else to be done. Come on, Miz Kincaid. Let's go see if your breakfast is done. You hear of any market for this old junk, you let me know, all right?"

She nodded and Paddy headed for the door. But Perrie lingered for a moment longer. The scent of ink still permeated the room, even after nearly fifty years. She closed her eyes and her thoughts drifted back to the little print shop she'd loved when she was a kid. It was because of that place that she'd become a reporter.

For an instant, she wished Joe was with her. She wanted to share this with him, the same way he'd shared the wolves with her, telling him about the first time she'd realized she wanted to be a newspaper-woman. And then she remembered how things had been left between them.

They were like a pair of magnets, at times attracted

and at other times repelled by each other. She could understand the latter. But where did the attraction come from? Sure, he was handsome, but she'd never been hung up on physical attributes. She assumed he was intelligent, although she had never carried on a scholarly conversation with him. He was definitely charming, the type of man that most women found irresistible.

Maybe it was something else, something less obvious. Though he was friendly enough, he always seemed to stop short of any shared intimacy. Most men she'd known could talk for hours about themselves, but she hadn't managed to get a single iota of personal information out of Brennan beyond his revelation about his debt to Milt Freeman. When she questioned him, he just brushed her curiosity off with a clever quip or a teasing remark.

Perrie would hazard a guess that there hadn't been a woman on the planet who had managed to get inside Joe Brennan's head—or inside his heart. She wouldn't be the first—and she didn't want to be.

7

THE WOODS WERE DARK and silent when she returned home, the soft crunch of her boots echoing off the tall trees and disappearing into the night. Perrie had spent the entire day away from Bachelor Creek Lodge, simply to avoid seeing Joe again. Breakfast at Doyle's, lunch with the brides and practice for the games after that. She even spent an hour before dinner above Doyle's, reexamining what was left of the *Muleshoe Monitor*.

She wasn't really angry with Joe. But she wasn't ready to forgive him yet, either. One step toward a truce usually resulted in another step backward. Why couldn't they just get along? She was stuck here in Alaska for who knows how much longer, forced to see him every day, whether she wanted to or not. The least he could do was leave her in peace.

But did she truly want that? More and more, she found herself looking forward to their time together. And even worse, she enjoyed the bantering, the arguments, the ongoing battle for control. Joe Brennan was the first man she'd ever met who didn't let her walk all over him.

She'd always been a single-minded person, a woman who made her opinions known. Men had been attracted to her in part because of her notoriety, her position as a successful reporter. But Joe was not part of her world; he lived outside the orbit of the *Seattle Star*. He didn't care that she was Perrie Kincaid, award-winning journalist. He knew her as Perrie Kincaid, pain in the butt, unhappy guest, woman with a single mission—to get out of Muleshoe, Alaska, at any cost.

But lately, she hadn't been as obsessed with escape as she had been when she'd arrived. During her training session this afternoon with the brides, she'd all but forgotten her reason for entering the games. Through all the snowshoeing and wood splitting and dogsledding, her thoughts were on Joe—on how she'd prove to him that she could handle the rigors of life in the wilderness.

Something had changed between them, a change so subtle she'd barely noticed it. Since their day with Romeo and Juliet, she'd begun to look at Joe Brennan as more than just a minor roadblock in her plans to write the Riordan story. He had wormed his way into her life, teasing and cajoling, challenging her at every turn. In her mind—and her heart—he'd become an incredibly sexy, attractive, intriguing man.

Perrie slowly pushed open the front door of her cabin, trying to push the tangle of thoughts aside, as well. Why couldn't she make sense of this? She'd always had such command over her feelings. But Joe Brennan defied every attempt she made to define her feelings, to restrain her fascination...to keep herself from falling head over heels for him.

As she stepped inside and closed the door against the cold, she noticed a small white envelope on the floor in front of her. Her heart skipped a beat. Could it be from Joe? But when she saw the childish scrawl on the outside, she scolded herself for such a ridiculous reaction.

With a tiny smile, she tugged a handmade Valentine from the envelope, realizing for the first time that Valentine's Day was coming up very soon. She'd never paid much attention to the holiday. Once she'd been transferred out of Lifestyles, she'd been spared the syrupy articles about hearts and flowers, sentiment and romance.

"Roses are red, violets are blue," Perrie read, "I'm happy to have a new friend like you. Sam." She traced her finger over the ragged letters of the little boy's name, a flood of affection filling her heart. She couldn't recall ever receiving a valentine before, beyond the little cards exchanged in grade school. No boy, or man, had ever taken the time to express his fondness for her in such a sweet way.

She leaned back against the door and closed her eyes. Now was not the time for regrets. She'd never had any real romance in her life. But she'd had professional success beyond her wildest dreams. Her work was so exhausting she'd never noticed the empty apartment she came home to night after night. Why did it suddenly seem that it wasn't enough? Why did she feel as if she deserved more?

Perrie slammed her fists back against the door, only to have the sound echo back at her. She jumped away from the door and another knock sounded from the other side of the rough planks.

"Perrie, I know you're in there. I've been waiting for you to get back. Open the door."

She reached for the knob, then pulled her hand back. Drawing a long breath, she cleared her mind of all her silly romantic notions about Joe Brennan, as if he would somehow be able to read her thoughts once she opened the door. But she didn't anticipate the tiny thrill that shot through her when she came face-to-face with the man once again.

He smiled at her, the soft spill of light from the inside

of the cabin illuminating the handsome planes and angles of his face. "Hi."

She couldn't help but return his smile. He had an uncanny way of soothing the tension between them, of charming away all the animosity with a teasing word or devilish grin. "Hi," she replied. It was all she could say with the breath left in her lungs.

What was wrong with her? She felt like a lovesick teenager. How could she have gone from complete frustration to heart-pounding attraction in the course of a single day? What had changed?

"Are we still mad at each other?" he asked.

Perrie sighed. Was it even possible to stay angry with Joe Brennan? She thought not. "No. I'll probably curse you up one side and down the other the next time I have to hike to the outhouse in the middle of the night, but for now, I'm feeling generous."

He reached out and grabbed her hand. "Good. Because I have something special I want to show you." He tugged her back outside the cabin, then pulled the door shut behind her.

"Where are we going?"

"Not far," he said.

He pulled a flashlight from the pocket of his jacket and they headed down a path that took them deeper into the woods. The tracks from the dogsled had packed the snow, and even in the dark, she knew they were headed toward the river.

They walked side by side, silent but for the sound of their boots against the snow. He held her hand, her bulky mitten firmly in his grasp, and when she slipped, he circled her shoulder with his arm, pulling her close.

It all seemed so natural between them, this casual touching, as if they'd crossed some invisible line in their relationship that allowed them to acknowledge their regard for each other. She liked the way it felt, his hands on her, yet with no sexual overtones.

"Are we almost there?"

"Almost," he said. "Stop right here."

She looked around but saw only what she'd seen for the last few minutes. Thick forest nearly obliterating the stars above. Snow on either side of the path, illuminated by the weak glow from his flashlight. "What is it?"

He stepped behind her and covered her eyes with one hand. He placed his other hand at her waist to steady her, then nudged her forward. "Just a few more yards," he said. "Don't be afraid. I won't let you fall."

"I—I'm not afraid," Perrie said softly.

When she'd taken the required number of steps, he stopped her, then slowly pulled his hand away. It took a moment for her vision to focus and then her breath caught in her throat.

They stood on the edge of the forest, overlooking the wide, frozen expanse of the Yukon. And there, in the northern sky, hung a kaleidoscope of swirling color, so strange and unearthly that she was afraid to breathe. Red, purple and blue washed the black horizon in brilliance, like a giant spirit rising up into the sky in a jeweled coat.

"I knew you'd want to see this," he said.

"I—I don't know what to say."

He wrapped his arms around her waist and pulled her back against his long, lean body. His chin rested on the top of her head. "You don't have to say anything. I wanted to be the one to show you."

"It's incredible."

"I've never seen an aurora this nice in the middle of winter. They usually occur in the fall and spring. But every so often, on a dark night in winter, the sky comes alive with light. You can almost feel it in the air."

"Do you know why they happen?" Perrie asked.

"Protons and electrons from sunspots start floating around in space," Joe explained, leaning over her shoulder until she could feel his warm breath on her face. "They get drawn into our atmosphere near the magnetic poles and they light up and dance and put on a show."

"Why didn't I notice it on the way home?"

"The headlights on the truck, the trees on either side of the road. Or maybe you just weren't looking."

Perrie turned around in his arms and stared up at him. She couldn't see his face in the darkness, but she wanted to believe he was looking down at her. "Thank you for bringing me here."

"I wanted to show it to you. I only wish you could see it from the air, because it's even more glorious. Maybe someday..." His voice drifted off when he realized, as she did, that there wouldn't be any "somedays" between them. "I thought you might write another story."

"I will," Perrie said.

They stood there for a long time, facing each other, Perrie imagining the strong features of his face, his chiseled jaw, which felt so good beneath her hands, and his mouth, as potent as aged brandy. She wanted him to kiss her, here and now, while they stood under this magical light. She wanted to wrap her arms around his neck and draw him close until all their thoughts became actions, words transformed into sweet taste and touch.

The intensity of her feelings took her by surprise. How could she have spent so many days with this man, yet never realized how she felt? A few days ago, she wanted nothing more than to put him out of her life. And now all she could think of was being near him.

She wanted him to kiss her, and hold her, and make love to her until the sun drove the colorful lights from the sky. The revelation sent a shiver through her and she trembled.

"You're cold," he said. "We should go back."

"All right," she said. As they retraced their path through the woods, Perrie's mind scrambled for a way to make this night last a little longer. She could grab Joe and kiss him, the same way she'd grabbed him that very first day in the truck, daring him to reveal his true feelings for her.

But she didn't want to force the issue. If Joe Brennan wanted her as much as she wanted him, then she would have to be patient. For the first time in her life, she didn't want the control. She needed Joe to take the first step.

But there had to be a way to encourage that, a way to show him how she felt. Perrie cleared her throat. "This was very thoughtful of you...Joe." His name didn't come naturally to her lips. She'd grown so used to calling him Brennan that "Joe" almost seemed like an intimacy reserved for lovers.

"You know there's nothing that says we can't be friends," he said, his attention still fixed on the path in front of them.

"What kind of friends?" Perrie asked.

"The kind that doesn't fight all the time?"

They reached the front porch of her cabin and he held tight to her hand as they climbed the slippery steps. "I'm sorry I've been so hard on you," she said. "I understand that you take your responsibility seriously." She opened the door and stepped inside, deliberately leaving the door wide in an unspoken invitation. To her relief, he followed her inside.

"And I can live with that," Perrie continued, shrugging out of her jacket. "If you can understand how important my job is to me. It's my whole life."

He took a step forward, then gazed down into her eyes. Gently, he drew his fingers along her cheek, and with a start, she realized that he'd removed his gloves. The contact sent a current of desire racing through her.

"There's more to your life than that, Perrie," he murmured.

She opened her mouth to contradict him, but the words that came out were not what she intended to say. "I want you to kiss me," she blurted. A flush of heat rising on her cheeks betrayed her mortification and she looked away, unable to meet his gaze.

He took her chin between his thumb and finger and forced her eyes back to his. "I want to kiss you."

But he didn't bend closer, didn't bring his lips down on hers. Instead, he slowly let his hands drift down from her face, running his fingers along her shoulders until his caress reached her breasts.

Perrie closed her eyes as he cupped the soft flesh in his palms, his warmth seeping through the layers of clothes until she could almost imagine his skin touching hers. She held her breath and he lingered there for a long time, teasing at her nipples until they were hard against his touch. When she opened her eyes again, he was staring down at her, his blue eyes glazed with unmistakable desire.

Slowly, the caress dropped lower, her skin tingling with every delicious inch. Her belly, her hips, her backside. And then he slipped his hands beneath the layers of sweaters she wore and began to work his way back up to where he began.

Still he didn't kiss her, though he moved close, his lips hovering over hers. His soft, uneven breathing was all that touched her mouth. His quiet words drifted into her consciousness. She tried to understand their meaning, then realized that they were as disjointed as her own murmured pleas.

Without his kiss, every sensation he created with his hands was more powerful, more deeply experienced, touching the very center of her soul. She wanted to tear her clothes off, and his, as well. And like the clothes they wore to protect against the cold, they'd been trapped under layers and layers of misunderstanding. She wanted to strip all that away, to find the real man beneath, alive with desire and vulnerable to her touch.

She reached out and unzipped his parka, then drew her hand along the front of his shirt. But when she moved to unfasten the top button, he stopped her, taking hold of her hand and bringing it to his lips.

He kissed her palm and each of her fingertips, then allowed her hand to drop to her side. "I'd better go," he murmured with a smile of regret.

"You—you don't have to go," Perrie said.

"Yes, I do. We just became friends, sweetheart. We can't become lovers in the same night." With that, he turned and opened the door, then walked out into the frozen night.

Perrie stood in the doorway, shivering in the cold, watching him make his way up to the lodge. When the frigid air finally cleared her senses, she began to realize what had passed between them. He wanted her as much as she wanted him. And the next time they were together, they would become lovers.

Perrie wrapped her arms around herself, a shudder of anticipation coursing through her limbs. For the first time since she'd arrived in Alaska, she didn't want to leave. She wanted to stay here at the lodge and learn what she already believed—that Joe Brennan would be an incredible lover.

"How DO YOU KNOW if you're in love?"

Perrie looked around the room at each of the brides. First Linda, who considered her question with great seriousness. Then Mary Ellen, whose dreamy look predicted a romantic, movie-inspired answer. And then Allison, whose idea of love probably changed as often as the weather.

The brides' cabin reflected the full glory of tomorrow's holiday. Bouquets of hothouse flowers decorated nearly every surface, and Perrie had learned that one of the bush pilots had made a special run to an Anchorage florist to fill all the orders from the town's bachelors.

Boxes of candy littered the coffee table, and other gifts and tokens of affection were scattered about the room. The brides were scheduled to go back home at the end of the month, and the competition for permanent companionship was heating up. After the Muleshoe Games, Perrie predicted that there would be a number of proposals made to each of the girls, though she wasn't sure whether they'd accept.

"I don't know if there's any way to explain it," Linda said. "I guess you just know when you know."

"Bells will go off inside your head," Mary Ellen said. "You'll feel all tingly and shaky and you'll see stars. Angels will sing."

Allison groaned. "That only happens in the movies, silly. The way I see it, it's possible to love almost any man, if you really want to."

"You mean if he's handsome enough, he doesn't wipe his nose on his sleeve, and he has enough money to keep you happy?" Linda asked.

Allison grinned. "That sums it up quite nicely."

"But there must be more," Perrie said. "I can't believe so many people in this world have fallen in love and they haven't written these things down somewhere."

"Is this for the story," Linda asked, "or are you interested for personal reasons?"

"For the story," Perrie lied, but she could tell Linda saw right through her. "All right. I may need the information in order to evaluate my growing feelings toward an...acquaintance."

"Hawk or Joe?" Allison asked. "And if you say Burdy, I'm going to scream."

"It's Joe. Although both Hawk and Burdy have been perfect gentlemen, sweet and accommodating, I seem to find myself attracted to the resident scoundrel. The man has dated every single woman in Alaska, he delights in making my life miserable, and he has absolutely no concern for my career." Perrie paused to reconsider what she was about to say. "And I think that—against all common sense—I might be in love with him."

They had spent nearly every minute together since their night with the northern lights. By day, he would take her to all his special places in and around Muleshoe. And in the evenings, they would sit in front of the fireplace in her cabin and talk. She would work on her stories and he would read them.

And later, as night closed in around them, they would kiss and touch. Although she'd been certain that they would become lovers, Joe had been careful not to push them forward too fast. Just when it seemed there would be nothing else to do but make love, Joe would smile sweetly and kiss her good-night, leaving her to wonder why he insisted on waiting.

Mary Ellen clapped her hands in delight, snapping

her back to reality. "Oh, that's so sweet! It's like destiny, isn't it? Like that old film with Cary Grant and that French actress. Only they met on a tropical island and this is Alaska. And he wasn't a pilot. But it was so romantic."

"Does he feel the same way about you?" Linda asked.

"I don't know," Perrie replied. "To be honest, I'm not real familiar with all of this. I mean, I've never been in love before. And I don't think any man has ever been in love with me. I've had relationships, but they've never made me feel this way."

"Joe Brennan is definitely a good catch," Allison said. "He's got a successful business, he's handsome, and I bet he kisses like a dream."

Perrie sighed. "Yeah, like a dream."

"What makes you think you're in love with him?" Linda asked.

"At first, I wasn't sure. But then, after I thought about it, I realized it was something really silly. That's why I wanted to ask you."

"It's his eyes, isn't it?" Allison asked. "He's got those incredible blue eyes."

"I bet it's because he's a pilot," Mary Ellen ventured. "Pilots are so dashing and brave."

"It's because he likes the way I write."

The three women stared at Perrie, a trio of confused expressions directed her way.

"I—I wrote this story about a family of wolves that he took me to see. And I combined it with a story about a family living in the bush. I didn't think it was anything special, but Joe thought it was. And now he takes me to all these special places and he asks me to write stories about them. And then we…read them together."

"That's it?" Allison asked.

"No, not completely. I've always worked hard at my job, but no matter what I accomplished, it never seemed to be enough. There was always this vague ambition that I had to satisfy, another goal just out of my reach. But when Joe says that he likes my stories, that's enough. That's all I really need. Suddenly a Pulitzer doesn't seem to matter anymore."

"He respects you," Linda said. "And he's proud of you. That's a wonderful thing."

Perrie smiled. "It is, isn't it? It's so strange, but I feel as long as he believes in me, that's enough." She ran her fingers through her hair and groaned. "At least, I think it is. How am I supposed to know? I've been away from my work for so long, I can't be sure. Maybe I don't love him at all. Maybe I'm just bored and he's a convenient distraction."

"You don't have to decide right away," Linda said. "You've got time."

"But I don't!" Perrie cried. "Sooner or later, I have to go home. I have a career to think about, and if I stay away much longer, I won't want to go back. What if I stay and then I find out I'm really not in love? Or what if I go back home and realize that I am?"

Mary Ellen reached over and patted Perrie's hand. "There, there, don't get so upset. I think you should follow your heart. When the time comes to decide, you'll know."

"She's right," Linda said. "Listen to your heart. Don't analyze this like one of your newspaper stories. Don't try to look for all the facts and figures. Just let it happen the way it happens."

Perrie nodded, then stood up. "All right, that's what I'll do. I'll listen to my heart." She walked over and grabbed her parka, then pulled it on. "I *can* listen to my heart. By the way, are there any new developments on the romance front for you three?"

"I've been seeing Luther Paulson," Linda said. "He's a really sweet man. So gentle and caring."

"George Koslowski has invited me to his place to watch movies tonight," Mary Ellen said. "He's got *Roman Holiday* on tape. Any man who loves Audrey Hepburn can't be all bad."

"And I've decided to pursue Paddy Doyle," Allison finished. "He's still a young man and he's got a successful business. He's handsome in a burly sort of way. And he's been widowed for two years. That's long enough."

Perrie nodded distractedly, her thoughts still on Joe Brennan. "That's nice," she murmured as she walked to the door. "I'll see you all at the games tomorrow."

She needed to be alone with her thoughts. As she walked down the main street of Muleshoe, she contemplated everything that the brides had said, and all that she'd told them. Now that she'd actually put words to her feelings, they didn't seem so confusing.

She was in love with Joe Brennan. And that was all she needed to know for now.

THE SUN GLEAMED off the snow, the reflection so bright that Joe had to shade his eyes to see beyond the lodge. In the distance, Perrie methodically split wood in front of the shed. Hawk had provided her with plenty of logs and a newly sharpened ax and she worked at the task with a single-minded intensity.

He had to admire her tenacity, even if he didn't approve of her purpose. Though she'd come a long way with her wilderness skills, he hadn't the heart to tell her that she probably couldn't win. Besides the three brides, there were four other single women who had lived in the area for years who coveted a weekend at the Hot Springs, all with finely honed talents.

Even if Perrie did manage to emerge victorious, he was still determined to protect her safety. The organizers of the Muleshoe Games had approached him about providing the air travel to Cooper and he'd accepted. Perrie was in for a surprise if she thought she'd make a clean getaway. If she went to Cooper, he'd go along. And he'd make sure that once they got there, she wouldn't want to leave the room.

Over the past few days, they'd connected in a way so unexpected that he wasn't sure what he was feeling. Every minute they spent together had brought them closer and closer. And now, he could barely imagine a day without her.

They had become friends, and soon they would become lovers. Every night, he had wanted to stay with her, to continue their sensual explorations. But as soon as he touched her in such intimate ways, he knew he was lost. The only way to halt the inevitable was to leave.

She wouldn't be like the others. When it finally happened between them, it would be something very special. And it would happen. Cold showers and pure thoughts could take him only so far. Sooner or later, his resolve would crumble and he'd give way to the desire that seemed to fill him every time he looked into her eyes.

Joe took another sip of his coffee, then tossed the rest over the porch railing and headed into the lodge. Julia was busy dusting the great room and she smiled as he walked through to the kitchen.

He filled his empty mug from the freshly brewed pot, glancing at the mess that Sammy had spread across the kitchen table. The little boy was so wrapped up in his own activities that he barely noticed Joe's presence.

"What are you up to, buddy?"

Sam chewed on his lower lip as he carefully wielded scissors on a large piece of construction paper. "I'm makin' a valentine for my mom."

Joe frowned. "Aren't you starting a little early?"

"Valentine's Day is tomorrow. I already made one for Perrie a few days ago. I put it under her door."

"Valentine's Day is tomorrow?"

"I bet you didn't get Perrie a present, did you?" Sam asked.

"I guess I didn't think of it."

"She's your girlfriend, isn't she?"

Joe considered the boy's question for a moment, then nodded. "Yeah, I guess she is. At least, I want her to be."

"Then you better show her how much you like her."

Joe sighed. It was already too late to get her a gift. Flowers weren't an option in the dead of winter, and with all the bachelors in town angling for the brides' good graces, he suspected that Weller's General Store would be sold out of anything resembling a romantic gift.

He needed something to show Perrie that he no longer thought of her as just a guest or an acquaintance or a constant intrusion in his life. That he'd found a place for her in his heart. That he cared for her more than any other woman he'd known.

"Maybe you could make me a valentine for Perrie?"

Sam sent him a sideways glance, then shook his head. "That wouldn't be right. You need to make it yourself. My mom says that if you make a gift yourself, that means it's from the heart."

Joe sat down next to Sam and picked up a paper doily. "Where do I start?"

Sam handed him scissors and a piece of construction paper. "Make a heart. Just fold it in half and cut it out. Then paste it on a doily. Girls like doilies."

"How do you know?"

Sam held one up and studied it. "It looks like ruffles and lace. Girls like that stuff. And they like glitter and these little round sparklies."

"Sequins?"

Sam nodded and pointed to the bottle of glue. "Paste 'em on with that."

Joe watched Sam put together his valentine and then began to work on his own. He hadn't touched paper and glue since he left grade school. The glue seemed to stick to everything, and before too long, he had sequins stuck to his palms and glitter under his fingernails.

"What are you going to write on it?" Sam asked, carefully observing Joe's progress.

"I thought I'd sign my name."

Sam slowly shook his head. "You gotta write something sweet and mushy. Or make up a poem. Girls like poetry."

"I'm not good at poetry."

"Then you have to tell her how beautiful she is. Say her skin is like rose petals or her lips taste like cherry soda."

Joe blinked in surprise. "That's pretty good. Can I use that?"

"You should think of something on your own. What do you want to say to her?"

Joe wanted to tell her how beautiful she was, how much he loved to be with her. He wanted to ask her to spend the night with him. But he couldn't put that on a valentine. "How about if I ask her to go to the dance at Doyle's?"

"That's good," Sam replied. "Girls like dancing."

"I'm going to have to remember these tips. Girls like doilies, sequins, poetry and dancing." Joe finished the valentine, then took a few moments to compose his message before he stepped to the kitchen sink to wash the glitter off his hands.

"Are you gonna give it to her now?"

"I thought I would. She's out practicing her wood splitting."

Sammy picked up his valentine and held it out in front of him. "Just remember," he said distractedly, "if she tries to kiss you, run away as fast as you can."

Joe wasn't about to follow that bit of Sam's advice. If Perrie did decide to kiss him, he'd probably drag her into the cabin and begin where they had left off the night before. He grabbed his valentine from the table and tucked it inside his jacket, then ruffled Sam's hair as he walked past. "Thanks for the help, buddy."

Joe found Perrie back at her cabin. She sat on the porch, her attention centered on adjusting the straps on her snowshoes. "How's the training going?"

She glanced up and he thought he detected a blush rise on her already rosy cheeks. Her smile warmed his blood and he bent down and kissed her mouth. Strange how kissing her felt so natural, how he barely had to think before he pressed his lips to hers.

"I can't seem to get this strap right."

"Here, let me see." He took the snowshoe from her and carefully readjusted the strap. "How's that?"

"Why are you doing this? I thought you'd be the last person to help me."

"If you're going to compete, you should do your best."

"Do you really mean that?"

"Yes," Joe said, knowing the truth in his words. "I'd like to see you leave all those wimpy brides in the dust."

Her green eyes sparkled with surprise. "I'm getting really good at the wood splitting. I'm still a little shaky on the snowshoes, but I think, with Hawk's dog team, I've got the mushing competition sewn up."

"Did you know there's a dance at Doyle's after the games are over?"

She sent him a curious glance, the corners of her mouth quirking up. "I heard something about that."

Joe withdrew the valentine from his jacket and held it out to her. He didn't know what to say. To tell the truth, he felt a little silly handing her a handmade card. But all his reservations dissolved at the tender smile she gave him. He said a silent thank-you for Sam's advice, then sat down beside her on the steps.

"You made this yourself?"

"With some advice from Sam. He told me not to let you kiss me."

Perrie laughed. "You're taking your cues from a nine-year-old?"

Joe bumped against her shoulder playfully. "So, will you go to the dance with me, Kincaid?"

"Only if you kiss me again," Perrie teased.

He leaned closer, their noses nearly touching. "I think that could be arranged."

He kissed her then, a soft, simple kiss. He didn't know such an innocent act could bring such a powerful reaction. Desire flooded his senses and every thought dissolved in his mind until all he was conscious of was the feel of her lips on his. Her mouth was so sweet; he had become addicted to the taste, needing more and more.

Then she drew back, her gaze fixed on his mouth. "I'll go to the party at Doyle's with you," she murmured.

"Good," Joe said. He pushed to his feet, then brushed the snow from the back of his jeans. "I guess I'll see you after the competition."

"We aren't going to see each other tonight?"

He reached out and cupped her cheek in his palm. "Sweetheart, I think you better get some rest tonight."

"All right," Perrie said. "It's a date. I'll see you tomorrow."

Joe shoved his hands in the back pockets of his jeans and nodded. "Yeah, a date. I'll come down tomorrow morning and get you. We'll ride into Muleshoe together."

"That would be nice," Perrie said.

He whistled a cheery tune as he walked back down the path to the lodge. He'd never really set much store in romance. But he had to admit that a handmade valentine had touched Perrie's heart. His mind flashed an image of her reaction and he smiled to himself.

He was through with waiting. The next time he touched Perrie Kincaid, he wouldn't stop until every desire, every secret fantasy they shared had been completely satisfied.

8

EVERY PERSON IN MULESHOE, from the smallest child to the town's oldest citizen, one-hundred-year-old prospector Ed Bert Jarvis, gathered on Main Street to watch the games. In the middle of a long winter, any social activity was hailed as an "event." And this year's event was even more special.

Ed Bert, born in the year of Muleshoe's "boom," served as the grand marshal of the parade, a ragtag collection of decorated pickup trucks, dogsleds, snowmobiles and a pair of bicycles. They were accompanied by the town band, which consisted of Wally Weller on trumpet, his wife, Louise, on saxophone, and son, Wally Jr., on drums.

Perrie had never seen anything like it. Though the temperature still hovered around zero, no one seemed to notice. Fur parkas and mukluks were standard uniform for half the population, while the more stylish half chose down jackets and Sorel boots. No one stayed home.

She'd convinced Paddy Doyle to cover the event as a stringer for the *Seattle Star*. The barkeeper wandered around with his camera, hoping to find a few good shots to accompany Perrie's article on the mail-order brides and boasting about the press pass that she'd clipped to his collar.

The brides' competition had been scheduled for mid-afternoon, the final event after the general competition for the townsfolk. Contests of strength and speed were interspersed with a bed race, an ice-carving contest and an event that involved stuffing as many pickled eggs into a competitor's mouth as humanly possible.

To Perrie's surprise, the three brides from Seattle hadn't offered much competition in the snowshoe race. They had all dropped to the rear of the pack and watched excitedly as Perrie and four other women raced ahead. The four other competitors, all longtime Alaskan residents, hadn't entered to find a husband. Like Perrie, they were after the first prize.

Perrie managed to finish third behind a pair of sisters, trappers who ran their own mitten-sewing business from a cabin ten miles from town. They were stout women without Perrie's quickness. But then, they spent most of the winter walking around in snowshoes.

To Perrie's surprise, Joe met her at the finish line, offering words of encouragement as he helped her unstrap her snowshoes. Hawk joined them, and as the trio headed over to hitch up the dogs, both men gave her more advice on proper race strategy.

The dogsled competition was Perrie's best chance at a win. Hawk had informed her that his dogs were the fastest and best trained of all the teams. To add a measure of safety, the women didn't race together. Instead they covered a course of nearly a mile that wove in and out of town and were timed from start to finish.

Perrie nervously waited at the starting line, trying to keep the dogs from bolting in the excitement. Joe stood at the head of the team, hanging tight to Loki's collar. He sent Perrie a confident smile and a wink as she listened to Hawk's simple instructions.

"Don't let the team get away from you," he said.

"You're always in control. Anticipate the turns and make sure the dogs are ready. Then balance yourself."

Perrie glanced over at the woman who held the fastest time so far, a tall, slender competitor in her early forties whose brother had once raced in the Iditarod. "She was fast," Perrie murmured.

"She was smart," Hawk countered as he stepped away from the sled. "But you're faster."

Joe let go of Loki's collar and joined Hawk on the sidelines. "Go get 'em, Kincaid."

Perrie took a deep breath and waited for the starter's gun. At the sound, she yanked out the snow hook and urged the dogs on, running behind the sled for the first twenty yards. In her nervousness, she nearly tripped and fell, but she gathered her composure and hopped on the back of the sled just in time to make the first turn off Main Street.

"Mush, boys," she called, her voice gaining confidence as the sled gained speed. "Come on, boys, mush!"

The race seemed to pass in a blur, the wind cold on her face and her breath coming in short gasps. The dogs responded well, as if their pride were at stake along with Perrie's. Loki anticipated each command and Perrie's turns were smooth and easy. When she reached the final straightaway, Perrie urged them on and she nearly flew down the snow-packed street.

She crossed the finish line to a rousing cheer from the crowd, then instantly forgot the command to stop the sled. Panicked, she shouted to the dogs as they ran right through a small crowd of onlookers beyond the finish line. Now that she'd given them a chance to run, they didn't want to stop.

She saw Joe's face pass by and wondered if the dogs would continue running until they got back to the lodge.

Finally a voice boomed over the crowd. "Ho, Loki, ho!" Hawk called.

"Ho, Loki," Perrie cried. "Ho, damn it, ho!"

The dogs slowed, then stopped, and she tumbled off the back of the sled into the snow. A few moments later, Joe knelt down beside her, laughing and brushing the snow off her face.

"Are you all right?"

"I feel like an idiot," Perrie muttered, sitting up. "I couldn't remember how to stop them."

"Well, lucky for you, they don't take off points for style. You gave the crowd a decent laugh."

Perrie groaned and lay back down in the snow. "How badly did I do?"

Joe bent down over her and grinned. "You've got the best time so far. And the Seattle brides are the only ones left to race. Come on, get up. You need some rest before the wood-splitting competition if you're gonna win this thing. Hawk will tend to the dogs. I'll buy you a hot cocoa and we'll discuss your strategy."

She let him pull her to her feet and he slipped his arm around her waist as they trudged back toward the crowd. Several of the town's single men came up to her to congratulate her on her time and inquire if she planned to attend the dance at Doyle's. She smiled and nodded, too exhausted to speak.

"I suspect your dance card will be full tonight," Joe said in a tone that barely hid his irritation.

"Jealous?" she asked, wincing at a cramp in her foot.

"Of those guys?"

"You hold a rather high opinion of your charms, Brennan."

He pulled her closer. "I happen to know that my charms don't work on you. I'm just saying that if you do manage to win this competition, I can guarantee that you'll have more than a few proposals to consider before the evening's done—both decent and indecent."

"And what kind of proposal are you planning to make?"

He stopped and looked down at her, his eyebrow cocked up in surprise. "That depends," he said slowly, "on what kind of proposal you'll accept."

Perrie knew where this bantering was leading and she wasn't sure what to reply. Ever since Joe had first touched her that night in her cabin, she'd thought of nothing else but what might happen the next time they were together. Would they make love? Or would something push them apart again, some doubt or misunderstanding?

And if they made love, what then? Would she wave goodbye and return to Seattle, filing Joe in among all the failed relationships and forgotten lovers in her past?

Perrie forced a smile and turned her attention to the crowd. What other choice did she have? It was clear that she couldn't stay in Alaska. She had a successful career waiting for her in Seattle. Besides, she'd been told over and over again that Joe Brennan was not the type to seek a permanent relationship. And neither was she. Even if she wanted to love him, she wouldn't let herself.

Whatever had begun between them would have to end on the day she left Muleshoe. They could continue this little dance of theirs, maybe even make love, but sooner or later she would say goodbye. And knowing Joe Brennan, he'd move on to the next available woman.

The thought of Joe with another woman brought her own twinges of jealousy, but she pushed them aside. Falling in love with him would be nothing but disastrous. And allowing herself any regrets about what they might or might not do would only add to the mess. She could make love to Joe Brennan and then leave him. She could and she would.

"Do you think I can win the wood-splitting competition?" Perrie asked, anxious to put their conversation back on a more benign track.

"Sweetheart, I think you could do just about anything you set your mind to."

Perrie bit back a curse. Every time she thought she'd figured Joe Brennan out, he would say something that made her lose all her resolve. How the hell was she supposed to keep herself from loving him when he called her sweetheart and told her he loved her writing and touched her until her blood felt like liquid fire?

They drank hot chocolate and waited as the rest of the brides finished the dogsled race. As Joe predicted, she came out the winner and currently led in the point total. But it was plain to see that three other competitors had a distinct advantage over her in the ax-wielding department—mainly due to biceps the size of tree trunks.

When the wood-splitting competition was ready to begin, Joe accompanied her to her spot, then gave her a quick peck on the cheek, causing a major reaction with the crowd.

"We can see you got yer bride all picked out, Brennan!" someone shouted. "That legend is at work again!"

Perrie could only force a smile as a flush of embarrassment warmed her face. But Joe merely laughed and waved at them, taking the teasing with his usual good nature.

"Don't hurry," he said. "Just do your best."

"I'm never going to win. Look at those women! They could bench-press a Buick."

"Yeah, but you're much prettier, sweetheart. In fact, if

they had a 'pretty' competition, you'd win hands down." With that, he turned and left her to stand in front of the crowd with the other seven single women. A tiny smile touched her lips and she picked up the ax and hefted it up to her shoulder.

She'd have three minutes to split as much wood as she could. And the rest of the day to savor the fact that Joe thought she was pretty.

The whistle sounded and she carefully set a log on end and raised the ax. Her aim was true and the wood cracked. A few more raps with the ax and one log became two and she repeated the process. Three minutes seemed like three hours, and before long, she could barely lift the ax, much less hit the log. Her arms burned and her back ached, and finally, when she thought she might just fall over from the pain, the whistle sounded again.

The crowd erupted in cheers and she collapsed on top of the woodpile. She watched as the judges worked their way down the line, counting the number of logs split. When they reached her, she rolled off the pile of logs and rubbed her sore arms.

In the end, one of the Alaskan Amazons won the wood-chopping contest. She wearily pushed to her feet and began to scan the crowd for Joe, when the judges returned to her spot and placed a huge medallion around her neck. At first, she wasn't sure what it all meant, and Joe added to her confusion when he grabbed her and spun her around.

"You won, Kincaid!"

"I placed fourth," Perrie gasped, grabbing hold of his arms.

"No, you won. The whole thing. You had the most points."

Perrie gasped. "I won?"

Ed Bert Jarvis shuffled over and pushed an envelope under her nose. "Here's yer prize, missy. Congratulations."

Perrie squirmed out of Joe's arms and snatched the envelope from the old prospector's hand. "I won the trip to Cooper?"

"You did."

Perrie screamed and waved the envelope at Joe. "I won, I won. I'm going to Cooper!" She threw her arms around his neck and hugged him hard. Then she looked up at him. His blue eyes darkened slightly before he brought his mouth down on hers.

He kissed her long and hard and deep. The crowd screamed its approval, but this time Perrie wasn't embarrassed at all. She tipped her head back and laughed. She'd conquered the wilderness and she'd proved to Joe Brennan that she could handle anything Alaska tossed her way. She was going to Cooper. In no time, she'd be back in Seattle.

The only problem was that she didn't want to leave Alaska. There was one more thing she needed to conquer...and he was kissing her at this very moment.

DOYLE'S WAS PACKED when they arrived. Music blared from the jukebox, mixing with the chatter of the crowd. Joe held tight to her hand as he led her through the press of people. He hadn't let go of her hand since he'd kissed her in front of the entire town. Odd, how they'd suddenly become an item. Everyone now looked at them differently, as if they belonged together.

Did people believe they were already lovers? Did they think he might actually be in love with her? Or did they all think that she was just another one of Joe Brennan's conquests? She shouldn't care what anyone thought, but she did.

As they made their way through the room, she had to stop time and time again while the townsfolk congratulated her on her win. Finally, when she met up with the brides, Joe disentangled their fingers and continued walking toward the bar.

"He looks positively besotted," Allison said, envy filling her voice. "I don't know how you do it. You weren't even looking for a man when you came here and you end up snagging the cutest bachelor in town."

"I haven't snagged him," Perrie said, uncomfortable with the notion. It wasn't as if she wanted to marry him...although the thought might have crossed her mind once or twice.

Didn't every woman think about marriage, about a husband and children at least once in her life? So what was it about Joe that summoned such ridiculous thoughts? She'd dated men much more suitable—stable, trustworthy men with good careers and monogamous personalities.

Boring men, she thought to herself. Safe men. That was one characteristic that she could never apply to Joe Brennan. He was the most dangerous man she'd ever met. Maybe that's what she found so alluring, the danger that he might just break her heart. She'd been throwing herself in harm's way her entire career, and now she'd moved the danger from her professional life to her personal life.

"Well, you sure proved you fit in up here," Linda said, giving her a hug. "I can't believe you won the dog-sled race. I fell off three times. And Mary Ellen didn't even get on. The sled ran off without her."

"I had good training," Perrie said, glancing over at Joe

and Hawk as they leaned against the bar. She distractedly listened to the brides' conversation, adding a comment here and there to appear interested. But all she was
really thinking about was how long it would take before
she and Joe were alone.

She caught his eye and gave him a little wave. With a
grin, Joe turned to take a bottle from the bar, then made
his way back to her. When he finally stood by her side,
he wove his fingers through hers. The contact made her
heart skip and start again.

"Come on," he said, leaning close. "There's an empty
table over there."

He nodded to the brides, then led her away. When
they reached a table in a dark corner, he pulled out her
chair with unexpected gallantry, then produced a bottle
of champagne from behind his back. Two wineglasses
appeared from his jacket pockets and he placed them on
the center of the table.

"Champagne?" she asked as she tugged off her jacket.

"We're celebrating," he said, sitting down across from
her and tossing his own jacket across the back of a chair.
He worked at the cork for a moment, then it popped off,
champagne bubbling out of the bottle. "It's not Cristal,
but it's the best Paddy has to offer."

He poured her a glass and then filled his halfway. "To
the most determined woman I've ever met," he said,
touching his glass to hers.

She smiled, then sipped at the champagne as she
scanned the crowd. Everywhere she looked, she found
men staring back. At first she smiled, but then she
started to feel a bit uneasy. She took a gulp of champagne. "Why are they all looking at me?"

Joe leaned back in his chair. "They're wondering if
they should come over and ask you to dance."

"But they asked me to dance the night I arrived here. What are they afraid of?"

"Now they think you're with me."

The bubbles from her champagne went down the wrong way and she coughed. "Am—am I with you, Brennan?" she asked, her eyes watering.

"You could call me Joe," he teased. "I think we know each other well enough, don't you, Perrie?"

"Am I with you, Joe?"

He gazed into her eyes for a long time, his devilish smile sending her back for another gulp of champagne. "Yeah, you are." He laughed. "You were amazing today, Perrie. I really didn't think you could do it, but you did."

"I guess you underestimated me," Perrie said, tipping her chin up stubbornly.

"I have a nasty habit of doing that," he replied. "In more ways than one." Joe reached over and took her empty glass from her hand. "Would you like to dance?"

Perrie nodded, wondering what he meant by his comment. How had he underestimated her? Was he still afraid that she'd plan an escape while she was in Cooper? Cooper Hot Springs was only a short distance from Fairbanks. Surely she could find a pilot to fly her to the airport. One phone call to her mother and a promise to appear at Sunday dinner would secure her a plane ticket.

Although, if her mother knew she'd met a man in Alaska, the plane ticket would not be forthcoming. Her mother's fondest wish was for a son-in-law. A doctor or dentist. She'd probably even settle for a pilot, as long as he was capable of fathering her grandchildren.

The dance floor was crowded, but Joe found them a small spot and pulled her close. A country-and-western tune wailed in the background and he pressed his body along hers and began to move with the music.

He really was a good dancer. The first time she'd danced with him she'd been surprised. But now, he held her differently, more intimately, and dancing with Joe took on a whole new meaning.

She wanted to seduce him, to tease and taunt him with her body, to lead him where she wanted him to go. The glass of champagne she'd guzzled emboldened her and she wrapped her arms around his neck and pressed her hips into his.

Perrie had never tried to deliberately seduce a man. She wasn't even certain she knew how. But instinct overcame insecurity and she simply moved with the music, nuzzling her face into the soft flannel of his shirt.

A soft groan rumbled in his throat and she felt his heartbeat, strong and sure, as she let her hand drift over the hard contours of his chest. They made a slow circle around the dance floor, yet she didn't notice any of the other dancers. The music and the noise and the people seemed to recede into the distance and all she could hear was Joe's gentle breathing against her ear.

Her fingers clutched at the front of his shirt and she pressed her forehead into his chest. Why was there always flannel between them? Why couldn't she have met Joe on some tropical island where the men barely wore clothes? Then she'd be free to touch him in all the ways she wanted.

The music stopped, but they kept on dancing, ignoring the silence between the songs. Somewhere during the long string of records, their dance became more intimate, a prelude to something new and exciting. She wished them to a different place where only silence would accompany their movements, but the jukebox still played and the people still shouted.

Perrie risked a glance up at him and their gazes locked. The passion in his eyes caused her heart to lurch. He pulled her hips tight against his, and his desire, hard and hot, branded her flesh through the fabric of her jeans. His meaning was clear. He wanted her as much as she wanted him, and nothing would stand in their way.

"So what's going to happen tonight, Perrie?"

"I don't know. But whatever it is, it's not going to happen here."

He grinned. "Then I think we'd better leave."

Before she could say another word, he left her on the dance floor, weaving his way to their table. An instant later, he was back with their jackets. He helped her slip into hers, then took her hand and led her to the door.

As soon as they got outside, he grabbed her around the waist and pressed her up against the brick wall near the door. His mouth ravaged hers, his hands desperately searching for soft, warm flesh beneath her sweater. He pulled her leg up against his hip and rocked against her until she could imagine him above her and inside of her.

"I want to love you, Perrie," he murmured, biting the tender skin in the curve of her neck.

She furrowed her fingers through his hair and pulled his head back. "Then take me home," she challenged.

WITH A CURSE, Joe frantically rummaged through the junk in his bedside table at the lodge. Why hadn't he planned ahead? The instant he'd opened the front door of Perrie's cabin, he knew he'd forgotten something. And now, the first time he was making love to a woman he truly loved, he hadn't come prepared.

He froze, stunned by his thoughts. No, it couldn't be.

The words just slipped into his head by mistake. But he'd never, ever used those words before. "I love Perrie Kincaid," he said slowly, testing each syllable as it formed on his lips.

Saying it out loud was all it took to realize that he spoke the truth. He loved Perrie Kincaid. And tonight, for the first time in his life, he'd truly make love to a woman. He would hold her in his arms and he'd never have to leave. He'd never wonder when—or how badly—the whole thing would end. He loved Perrie Kincaid.

A soft knock sounded on his bedroom door and Tanner called his name from the other side. When he replied, his buddy pushed the door open a crack. "You're back early," he said with a smile. "I thought you and Perrie would be out all night celebrating."

"We are," he replied, shoving the bedside drawer shut. "She's waiting for me up at her cabin. What are you doing back so soon?"

"Sammy was exhausted. And these days Julia is feeling a little tired, as well."

"Is she all right?" Joe asked. "She's not sick, is she?"

"She's pregnant," Tanner said.

Joe gasped and his jaw dropped. "You and Julia..."

"No, Burdy and Julia," Tanner teased. "Of course me and Julia. We've wanted to tell you since we got back, but you've been impossible to pin down. You've been spending so much time with Perrie."

Joe rose from the bed and walked to the door, then pulled Tanner into his arms and pounded his back. "I'm so happy for you," he murmured. "You and Julia deserve all the best. And so does Sammy. Jeez, Tanner, you're going to be a father. Hell, you're already a father. You and Sammy are great together."

"And what about you?" Tanner asked. "It wasn't hard to see what was going on with you and Perrie."

He turned away to pace the room. "I was just thinking about that." Joe paused, but the words were no longer difficult to say. "I love her. I've never felt like this before, and believe me, I'm as surprised as anyone. But she is the best thing that ever happened to me. She's obstinate and impertinent and opinionated. And she never backs away from an argument or a challenge."

"These are her good qualities?"

"Yeah," Joe said with a laugh. "And she's sweet and caring and she's got a talent for writing that I've never seen before. She's so smart. I can talk to Perrie about anything. And she can see right into my head and know what I'm thinking. I can't fool her." Joe sighed. "She's not easy, but that only makes me want her more."

"What are you going to do?"

"I haven't gotten that far yet."

"Well, you'd better think quick. There was a phone call for Perrie earlier this evening. Her boss called. I guess it's all right for her to go back to Seattle."

Joe closed his eyes and cursed, raking his fingers through his hair. "Great. I finally realize I love her and she's going to go home the minute she hears."

"Is she? Are you sure about that?"

"That's all she's wanted from the day she got here," Joe said. "You don't know Perrie. Even if she did love me, she'd never admit it. That stubborn pride of hers wouldn't allow it."

"You're going to have to give her the phone message. And you're going to have to tell her how you feel."

"Which first? The trick is in the timing," Joe said. "Will she love me or will she leave me?"

Tanner chuckled. "I guess that's up to you. You give

her a good enough reason to stay and she will." That said, Tanner stepped out of the room and closed the door behind him, leaving Joe alone with his thoughts.

How could he be so sure of his own feelings and not have a clue about Perrie's? She was attracted to him, but was it only physical? Would she take what she wanted and then walk away? Such poetic justice, to finally fall in love and then be forced to take a taste of his own medicine.

Joe grabbed the box from the bedside table and shoved it in his jacket pocket. He wasn't going to get any answers sitting alone in his bedroom. All the answers he wanted were waiting with Perrie.

He strode through the lodge and out the front door, his thoughts focused on only one thing. He'd tell Perrie how he felt and then he'd tell her about Milt's call...and then he'd wait for her reaction. He wouldn't have to wait long. Perrie wasn't one to keep her feelings to herself.

The distance between the lodge and her cabin was covered in record time. When he opened the front door, he expected her to be waiting for him where he'd left her, standing near the door. But then he realized how long he'd been gone.

Her jacket was tossed on the floor, followed by her mittens and hat. His gaze traced the path of mukluks, sweater and jeans to the bed. Slowly, he crossed the room to find Perrie, dressed in her T-shirt, curled up beneath the covers of the bed, sound asleep.

Joe knelt down beside the bed and studied her face. Her cheeks were still pink from the cold and her hair tumbled around her face. Long lashes, dark against her skin, fluttered faintly, as if she were struggling to escape the bonds of sleep. He leaned over and kissed her. His gaze stopped on her arm and he fought back a flood of anger at the person who had come so close to taking her life. He ran his fingers along the ragged red mark.

She opened her eyes and smiled at him sleepily. "I'm sorry. You were gone so long. And I was so tired."

"I should go and let you sleep. You've had a busy day."

She reached out and placed her palm on his cheek. "I want you to stay." She wriggled over on the bed and patted her hand beside her, a silent invitation to join her.

Joe pulled off his jacket and tossed it on the floor beside her clothes, then kicked off his boots. The bed gave beneath him as he crawled in beside her. He bent over her, his head braced on his elbow, and slowly traced the shape of her mouth with his thumb. A tiny smile touched her lips and then she kissed his fingers.

Desire flooded his senses, overwhelming in its intensity, and he pulled her beneath him, settling his hips against hers, his hands braced on either side of her head. She was warm and vulnerable, and with every kiss, he could feel her need growing to match his.

Every touch, every sigh were perfection, and he realized that loving her had become more than just words. He loved her with his mouth and his hands, and everywhere he touched, she came alive beneath him. He wanted to know every intimate inch of her body, he wanted to be able to understand her sighs and moans, the fleeting expressions that crossed her face.

The quilt tangled around them, and he muttered impatiently, unable to free her or himself. Finally, he pulled it from between them and she smiled. "I'm not cold anymore," she murmured, her eyes half-closed. "Are you?"

They lay side by side, foreheads pressed together. "Sweetheart, I'm warm. Very warm."

She toyed with the buttons of his flannel shirt. "Then help me take this off."

He growled and sat up, tearing off his shirt and the thermal underwear beneath. The touch of her hand sent a shiver racing through him. He watched as she smoothed her palm over his bare chest, her fingers like silk, teasing at the line of hair that ran from his collarbone to the button of his jeans. When her touch wandered below his waist, his jaw tensed and he pinned her hand behind her.

She was all soft flesh and gentle curves, and his palm pushed beneath her T-shirt. Her shoulders, her breasts, her belly, her hips. Before the night was through, he would memorize every inch of her. And if she ever left him, he would be able to close his eyes and remember each detail. But he wouldn't let her leave. He would make love to her and, in their passion, they would form an unbreakable bond.

Somehow, she managed to wriggle out of her T-shirt, and Joe's breath froze in his throat when he saw that she wore nothing beneath. He closed his eyes and nuzzled her neck, then slowly worked his way down, biting, nibbling, until his mouth closed over a taut nipple.

She murmured his name and twisted beneath him, furrowing her fingers through his hair. He felt such absolute power, yet at the same time such startling vulnerability. He could make her moan with pleasure and she could break his heart.

He kneaded her flat belly, moving lower and lower until his fingers found the silky scrap of her panties. Her breath was quick and shallow, every soft sound a frantic plea for more. He slipped his hand beneath the lace and touched her, and she cried out again and arched her back.

"You feel so good," he whispered. "So good."

"So good," she repeated. Perrie drew a ragged breath. "Oh, what are you doing to me?"

"Do you want me to stop, sweetheart?"

"No, no, don't stop. Touch me there. Just like that. Touch me there."

She pulsed with need, growing wetter beneath his fingers with every caress. He wanted to carry her to the edge and then catch her as she fell into sweet oblivion. He felt her tense and he knew she was near.

"Let go, Perrie," he murmured. "Let go. Let me love you."

Her breath suddenly stopped and he watched her face as a glorious expression of pleasure suffused her beauty. And then she shuddered and groaned and twisted beneath his hand. Wave after wave of ecstasy rocked her body and he held her close, whispering her name.

When she finally drifted back to reality, she released a weak breath and closed her eyes. He listened as her breathing slowed and her expression relaxed. He stared down at her lovely face, the color high, a sheen of perspiration dotting her forehead.

For a long time, he studied her, committing each feature to memory, burning an image of her into his brain. He closed his eyes and he could still see her, the face of an angel and the body of a goddess.

When he looked at her again, he saw that she was asleep. Joe touched his lips to her forehead, then pulled her body into his, nestling her backside against the nagging ache of his arousal. Wrapping his arms around her, he smiled. He held heaven in his arms and he wasn't going to let her go.

Tomorrow there would be time to say all that needed to be said, to tell her his feelings. To tell her about the phone call from Milt. But for now, none of that mattered. They'd finally found a place where pride gave way to passion, a place they might enjoy for a very long time to come.

9

SHE WOKE UP IN HIS ARMS, and for the first time in her life, Perrie felt utter contentment. The room had gone cold, the fire in the stove having burned to ash before sunrise. She snuggled beneath the quilts and listened to his breathing, deep and even and warm against the back of her neck. Seattle seemed so very far away...miles and miles and nearly a lifetime.

Here, with him, she felt safe and secure. Joe cared about her, he believed in her. And suddenly, she didn't have to work so hard to believe in herself. The pressure that weighed on her day-to-day life had disappeared. There were no thoughts of stories and deadlines and awards. Instead, her mind spun with images of exquisite tenderness and unfettered passion.

They hadn't made love last night, but they'd shared an incredibly intimate experience. She had given herself to him, stripped of all her inhibitions, vulnerable to his touch. And rather than feeling regret or embarrassment, Perrie felt sheer exhilaration. The world spun faster today, the sun shone brighter. Their lives together began when he took her to the edge and then caught her as she fell. And in his arms, she would be happier than she ever dared dream.

Like a cream-fed cat, she smiled and stretched. But his leg was thrown across her hips, the denim rough against her skin, and she couldn't move more than a few inches either way.

Perrie closed her eyes. For now, sleep was her only option, for she didn't want to wake him...not yet. She looked down at his arms, wrapped around her shoulders, strong and capable, and those hands that had worked such magic on her body. She wove her fingers through his and brought his hand to her mouth, kissing it softly. Who was this man who stirred such a deep desire in her? She barely knew him, yet she felt as if she'd known him her entire life.

Had destiny brought them together? She'd never believed in fate or karma, preferring logic and reason over all explanations. But something more powerful was at work here. If not for Tony Riordan and a stray bullet, she might have lived her entire life never knowing Joe Brennan. She might never have set foot in Alaska. And she might never have come to love a man the way she loved Joe.

The thought that they might never have met was unfathomable, and she drew a deep breath and banished it from her mind. She wasn't sure what the day would bring, but she had to believe that Joe felt the same way about her. And if he did, then her life would never be the same again.

A soft moan rumbled in her ear and Joe shifted and stretched behind her. She held her breath, but she could tell that he was awake, and she slowly turned around in his arms. He gazed down at her with half-hooded eyes and gave her a sleepy grin.

"You're still here," he murmured.

Perrie reached up and brushed a lock of hair from his forehead. "I could say the same of you."

He nuzzled her neck. "I can't think of any place I'd rather be. How about you?"

"I could think of lots of places, but I'd want you there with me."

"Where?" Joe asked.

"A big hotel with a big bed. And room service to cook us breakfast. Palm trees and sunshine and a beach towel for two."

He frowned. "Do you really hate the cold that much?"

"No," Perrie said. "I just hate all the clothes. And bundling up every time I need to go to the outhouse." She ran a playful finger down his bare chest. "And I like you much better without flannel and long underwear."

Joe smiled and kissed her on the tip of her nose. "So, when are you going to take your trip to Cooper?"

His question surprised Perrie. She'd forgotten all about her trip. And now that he brought it up, she wasn't sure what she was going to do with the prize. She had no intention of going back to Seattle before Milt called her. And Cooper was a long way from Muleshoe...and Joe. She couldn't imagine spending two hours, much less two days, away from him.

"I—I hadn't thought about it. Why do you ask?"

"I just thought you'd be anxious for a change of scenery. You've been stuck in Muleshoe for two weeks. And you worked so hard to win the trip."

Was he so eager for her to leave? She'd told him from the start that she'd use every option available to get back to Seattle. Did he still expect her to make a run for it? Was he hoping she would? "I suppose I should go soon. I'm not sure when Milt is going to call."

An odd look crossed his face, but it was gone before she had a chance to figure out what it meant. "Why don't you go today?" he suggested.

Perrie blinked in confusion. "Today? But isn't that a little soon? I mean, I'm not even sure if I can. There are reservations and the pilot and—"

He snuggled up to her and sighed. "Don't worry about the pilot. I'm the pilot," Joe said. "As for reservations, the resort doesn't see too many visitors this time of year. We'll probably have the place all to ourselves. It will be very romantic."

Perrie sat up in bed, pulling the sheet up around her chin. "You're the one who's supposed to fly me to Cooper? Since when?"

He stared up at her, his arm thrown across his forehead. "I've always been the one. I donated my services to the organizers of the games as soon as I found out you were entering the brides' competition. I wasn't about to take any chances."

Reality came crashing down around her and her dreamy state evaporated in an instant. How could she have been so foolish? She'd forgotten what had brought them together in the first place. Joe had a job to do, a favor to return. Was all this just part of the job? Had she somehow mistaken obligation for true emotion?

Perrie closed her eyes and calmed her scattered thoughts. This wasn't real, this life she and Joe had been sharing. She'd been swept away by silly schoolgirl fantasies of happily-ever-afters. Real was Seattle and her job.

"You wanted to make sure I didn't go back," she said, her voice deceptively even.

"At first...maybe. But you're not going back to Seattle. So we can turn this into a nice romantic weekend."

"Then you trust me?"

"Of course I trust you. Perrie, I only want you to be

safe. You understand that you're better off in Alaska with me, right?"

She didn't know what to say. She felt as if she were lost in the wilderness without a compass. All these feelings were so new and unfamiliar, she had no landmarks to keep her on course. Her whole life, she'd always been in control. But now she'd turned that control over to someone else, and it left her dazed and vulnerable.

Damn it, if she wanted to go home, she could. He had no right to stop her! After all, she was a grown woman, able to make all the choices in her life, including whether she wanted to risk that life to get a story or whether she wanted to take a chance with Joe Brennan. And he shouldn't have a thing to say about it.

Perrie calmly marshaled her composure. "All right," she said. "Let's go to Cooper. Today."

"We'll leave after lunch," Joe said, tugging her back down into the bed.

"No," Perrie replied. "I think we should leave now." She grabbed her T-shirt and yanked it over her tangled hair, then crawled out of bed. "I should pack. And you should go up to the lodge and get your things."

Joe grabbed her hand and pulled her down to sit on the edge of the bed. "What's the hurry? Come back to bed, sweetheart."

She stood up. "No, I think we should leave now."

With a groan, Joe rolled out of bed. Perrie tried to ignore the way his muscles bunched and rippled as he held his arms above his head and stretched. He raked his hands through his hair, then bent down and snatched up his shirt from the floor. "All right. I'll go throw some things in a bag and come back and get you in fifteen minutes."

He slipped his feet into his boots and shrugged into

his jacket before he grabbed her again and kissed her. "We're going to have a wonderful time," he murmured.

She watched him leave the cabin, then sat back down on the edge of the bed. Perrie pressed the heels of her hands to her temples. What was she doing? She had been in Muleshoe for two weeks. Long enough to forget all about why she was here in the first place. A story that had seemed so important suddenly didn't make any difference at all—and all because of one man. A man she barely knew.

And what had happened to her journalistic instincts? Why couldn't she read Joe Brennan's motives and feelings the way she was able to read so many others? He had to know that Cooper represented her only opportunity to escape, to get back to Seattle. He had to know she'd try. And when she did, would he stop her, or would he let her go?

Maybe this was just an easy way to end things between them. Over the past week they'd been nearly inseparable. Sooner or later, Perrie had expected some declaration of his feelings, but he hadn't said a word. Maybe he didn't have feelings for her. Or perhaps she was just another in a long line of women who blew in and out of his life like spindrift.

Perrie drew a deep breath. She would formulate a plan. They would go to Cooper and she would find a way to leave. And if he let her go, then she'd know he didn't care. And if he made her stay, then she would demand to know why. He would have to reveal his true feelings for her—or admit that he was only doing a job.

A shiver ran down her spine. It all came to this. All this love she felt for him was riding on the answer to an impossibly simple question: Would he stop her?

Suddenly, she didn't want to ask the question. If she

stayed in Cooper, she'd never need to know the answer. Perhaps it was unwise to force the issue, especially so soon. But then, the choice was bound to come up, for Milt would be calling her back to Seattle any day.

Somehow, it seemed easier this way. If he didn't want her, at least she wouldn't have to see it on his face. She'd walk out of his life without looking back. She would give them both a graceful exit.

Perrie stood up and rubbed the goose bumps from her arms. This was the right thing to do. She'd never been one to delay the inevitable. The sooner she knew, the sooner she could get on with the rest of her life.

The only problem was, she wanted the rest of her life to start now. And she wanted it to include Joe Brennan.

"I THINK WE SHOULD HAVE separate rooms."

Joe stopped short and looked at Perrie, not sure that he heard her right. They'd just arrived at the resort after an hour-long flight and Perrie had picked the last possible moment to drop her little bombshell. He knew something was bothering her for she'd been distant and uneasy since they'd left Muleshoe.

He thought she'd be happy that he had come along. After all, they'd spent so much time together in the past few days; he'd never considered that she might want to spend some time away from him. And after last night... What better place for them to be alone together but a beautiful resort in the middle of winter?

Sleigh rides, good food, dancing and the hot springs...indoor plumbing. He couldn't think of a more romantic place within a day's flight of Muleshoe.

But the trip *had* been hers, Joe mused, and he had essentially invited himself along. Maybe he was pushing too fast. Last night had been a huge step for them and he wouldn't be surprised if she harbored a few regrets. "Sure," he said. "Separate rooms are fine."

Perrie forced a grateful smile. "I mean, it's just that...well, we haven't really...and if we decide we don't want to, then—"

He reached out to stroke her cheek but drew his hand back before he touched her. "Perrie, it's all right."

"People might talk," she murmured, hoisting her shoulder bag up and starting toward the door.

Joe stared after her, shaking his head. If she really believed he bought that explanation, then he had some Alaskan swampland to sell her. It was obvious that she didn't want him along. When she won the prize, she assumed that she'd be going to Cooper Hot Springs with another pilot, one who wouldn't be watching her every minute of the day and night.

As he walked through the front door of the resort, realization hit him square in the face and he stopped, frozen in his tracks. She was planning to leave. Damn it, after all they'd been through, all that had happened between them, she was still determined to get back to Seattle.

Joe closed his eyes and tipped his head back, fighting the anger that bubbled up inside of him. Fine, he thought to himself. The hell if he was going to make her stay. Milt Freeman said it was safe for her to come back, so why not let her go? If Perrie could so easily throw away what they'd shared, then maybe it wasn't as special as he thought. She was just biding her time with him, waiting for the chance to get back to her real life.

Joe stepped up beside Perrie and filled out a registration card, signing his name with a frustrated flourish. Then he grabbed both of their keys and headed down the hall.

She caught up with him and touched his arm. "You understand, don't you?"

"Sure," Joe said. "This is your trip, not mine. In fact, if you want, I can fly back to Muleshoe right now."

His words seemed to take her by surprise, and for a second, he thought she might just accept his offer. "No, I'm glad you're here. Why don't we get unpacked and then we can get some lunch?"

Joe unlocked Perrie's room door and helped her carry her bags inside, tossing them on the bed. If she was determined to leave, he might as well make it easy for her. "Actually, I could use a shower," he said. "Why don't we meet in an hour? After we have lunch, we can try the hot springs."

Perrie nodded, then walked him to the door. "So I'll see you in an hour."

Joe stared down at her, wondering if this was the last time he'd ever look into her beautiful green eyes. Would she leave as soon as he was out of sight? He wanted to pull her into his arms and kiss her, to tell her that he was in love with her. But a strong instinct for self-preservation prevented him from saying anything. Time would tell if she really loved him.

He bent down and kissed her cheek. "All right, I'll see you later."

When he reached the privacy of his own room, Joe dropped his duffel on the floor and cursed softly. Leaning back against the door, he raked his hands through his hair. "The first woman I ever love and she doesn't love me," he muttered. "Serves you right, Brennan."

As he stood against the door, he heard a sound outside in the hall. He turned and peered through the peephole in the door. Perrie looked both ways, then headed down the hall. A cynical laugh escaped his throat and Joe opened the door to follow her.

A few minutes later, he stood in the shadows in a corner of the resort's lounge, his attention fixed on the transaction being negotiated at the bar. His jaw tensed and his heart hardened. He should have known she'd try. He should have known.

He watched as she spoke to the bartender before she moved down the row of chairs to a man who sat alone at the end of the bar. They talked for three or four minutes, Perrie glancing around the room every few seconds, as if she knew she was being watched. Then she shook his hand and hurried out of the bar, passing so close to Joe that he could nearly touch her, yet never noticing his presence.

Joe watched until she was long gone before he stepped from the shadows. In a few strides, he crossed the room and slid onto the stool next to Perrie's gentleman friend. He turned and glanced at the guy, who nursed a half glass of beer. "The woman. The pretty one with the red hair. What did she want?"

The guy scoffed. "What business is it of yours, buddy?"

Joe stared at him long and hard, wondering if he should grab him by the collar now or wait a few more seconds. He slowly stood and leaned over the guy. "It's my business, all right? Answer my question."

The guy shrugged, his cocky attitude cooled by Joe's thinly veiled temper. "She wants me to fly her to Seattle."

"Is she paying you?"

"She gave me a credit card number for starters. Said there would be an extra five hundred for me in Seattle if I was willing to wait for the cash."

"What's your name?" Joe asked.

"Andrews. Dave Andrews."

"I've heard of you. So, Andrews, if I check you and your plane out, am I going to be happy?"

"Hey, buddy, I'm a good pilot. And I keep my plane in top shape. You can ask any of the guys around here."

"When does she want you to fly her out?"

"Late this afternoon."

Joe reached in his pocket for his wallet, then withdrew two fifty-dollar bills. "Call her room and tell her you can't fly her out until tomorrow morning. She's in room 37."

"Who the hell are you?"

"The name's Brennan. Joe Brennan."

Andrews blinked in surprise. "Polar Bear Air? Aren't you the guy who found that climber on Denali a few weeks back?"

"Yeah, that's me."

Andrews smiled and clapped him on the shoulder. "I heard all about that. Good eyes. But if you want this lady to go back to Seattle tomorrow morning, why don't you just fly her yourself?"

"I'm not sure that she's going to leave," Joe replied. "I'm hoping she'll decide to stay. So if she doesn't meet you, I don't want you coming to look for her, all right?"

"But how am I gonna get paid?"

"I'll pay you."

Andrews considered the request for a moment, then nodded. "All right." He took a long swig of his beer. "What is this woman to you? Wife? Girlfriend?"

"I'm not sure yet. But I'm about to find out." Joe pushed away from the bar, then turned back. "One more thing. If she does leave with you, and she changes her mind, I want you to bring her back here. I don't care where you are, just turn around and fly her back. All right?"

"Man, you must have it real bad for this girl."

The man had a talent for stating the obvious. "You'll do it?" Joe asked.

Andrews nodded. "Yeah, if she wants to come back, I'll bring her."

"I'd appreciate that. Now call her and tell her the flight's been delayed."

Andrews nodded and asked the bartender for a phone. Satisfied that he'd covered all his bases, Joe turned and walked out of the lounge. But instead of returning to his room, he headed out the front doors of the lobby into the frigid cold.

This was a dangerous game he was playing, risking his heart on a woman he'd come to love. If he had any shred of common sense left, he'd walk away, save himself the pain and regret he was certain to feel. But his heart overruled his brain. He couldn't give up on them, not yet. He had to believe that somewhere in Perrie's heart she cared for him, maybe even loved him. And that given time, she'd recognize her feelings.

But did he have enough time? Or would the clock suddenly run out, leaving him with nothing but memories of a woman he'd loved and lost?

PERRIE STOOD NERVOUSLY in the hallway outside her room, watching as Joe pushed the room key into the lock. She knew this moment was coming, but she was completely unprepared to handle it.

She and Joe had spent a wonderful day together, swimming in the hot springs, enjoying a long, leisurely dinner and taking a sleigh ride through the snow-kissed woods. For brief snatches of time, she forgot all about

her plan to leave him and, instead, found herself capti-
vated by his charm and gentle humor.

All this would have been avoided, had her pilot kept
to their original plans. She would have left Joe waiting in
his room before dinner, while she flew away to the
safety of Seattle. Now she would have to wait until day-
break to make her escape.

Joe pushed the door open, then stepped aside. Perrie
slowly walked past him, silently rehearsing the excuse
she would give. She turned, but to her surprise, he was
standing right there, so close she could feel the heat from
his body.

In the blink of an eye, he pulled her against him and
captured her mouth with his. He kissed her long and
hard and she let him, knowing that it would be the last
thing they shared.

He pressed his forehead against hers and looked
down into her eyes. "You are so beautiful, Perrie. There
are times when I can't keep from touching you." With
gentle fingers, he brushed the hair from her temple, then
touched his warm lips to the spot. But he didn't kiss her
again. It was as if he were waiting for her to say something.

Drawing up her courage, Perrie smiled brightly and
stepped out of his embrace. "I—I'm really tired," she
said, inwardly cringing at the trite excuse. "I think I'd
like to turn in early." She swallowed hard. "Alone."

He showed no reaction to her words. In her heart, she
wanted him to brush away her excuse and carry her into
the room to make wild, passionate love to her against all
her protests. But Joe simply shrugged and smiled.

"I'm tired, too," he said, his gaze fixed on her face.

He stared at her a long time, as if he were memorizing
her features. And then he blinked and shook his head.

"Good night, sweetheart." He kissed her once more, a sweet and quiet kiss that nearly melted her icy resolve. She felt his fingers caress her cheek and then he was gone.

The sound of his room door closing drove a dagger into her heart and her breath caught in her chest at the pain. "Goodbye, Joe Brennan," she whispered, her throat tight with welling emotion.

The silence of her own room closed in around her. Perrie lay down on the bed and covered her eyes with her arms, willing away the doubt that assailed her mind. This was for the best. Even if they did love each other now, they would soon grow apart. To be together, one of them would have to give up their dream, and a sacrifice like that would soon cause regrets and recriminations.

Joe Brennan was a bush pilot in Alaska and Perrie Kincaid was a reporter in Seattle. Nothing they could do or say would change that fact. For them, love had been impossible from the beginning.

Perrie curled up on her side and stared at the bedside clock, counting the seconds for each minute that passed. Her eyes slowly closed, and soon she found herself floating between conscious thought and sleep.

Images of Joe drifted through her mind, but she didn't try to push them aside. She could almost feel his lips trace a path from her cheek to her mouth. She imagined the two of them at her door, imagined a different end to their time together. Her breath felt warm against his cheek and she listened, trying to make out the words she spoke. She pinched her eyes shut and focused her thoughts. And then, she heard herself.

I want you. I need you. I love you.

"I want you," Perrie murmured, opening her eyes. "I

need you." She pushed up from the bed. "And I love you."

A force more powerful than all her resolve pulled her toward the door. She opened it and stepped out into the hall, her gaze fixed on the room across from hers. Perrie reached out and touched the smooth wood, then, closing her eyes, she rapped hard.

The door swung open and he stood there, bare-chested, the light from his room gleaming off his smooth skin. "Perrie? Are you all right?"

"I—I want you," she murmured. "I need you. I—I—"

She tried to retreat but her feet were frozen to the floor. When she couldn't move, she closed her eyes instead, hoping that this was all part of her dream and would disappear in time. But then she felt his mouth on hers, the warmth of his lips, and she knew that she'd stumbled into something real.

He buried his face in the curve of her neck, and bent down, scooping her into his arms. This felt so right, so perfect, and no matter how Perrie tried, she couldn't make herself regret her decision. She and Joe belonged together, at least for this one night.

Joe kicked the door shut and leaned back against it. "I wanted you to come. I hoped you would." His mouth found hers again and he held her, enraptured, in a soul-shattering kiss.

He crossed the room, then gently placed her back on her feet. He gazed down into her eyes and she saw the desire there, dark and dangerous. If she touched him now, there would be nothing to stop them. And she didn't want to stop.

Slowly, she reached out and placed her palm on his chest. His heart beat strong beneath her fingers, quickening slightly as her hand drifted down to the waistband of his jeans, to the smooth ripple of his flat belly and then no further.

"Touch me," he said, his fingers furrowing through the hair at her nape.

She could hear the need in his voice, the urgency, and in that moment, she realized the power she had over him. He could no more resist than she could. They were both lost to this passion that raged between them. And whether it was born of love or lust, it didn't make any difference—it had to be satisfied.

Perrie splayed her fingers over the front of his jeans, tracing the hard ridge of his erection beneath the taut denim. He sucked in a sharp breath and moaned softly, a wordless plea for more. Emboldened, she stroked him, teasing him until he pushed her hand away.

As quickly as she had gained it, she lost her power and he took control. He tugged at her sweater and with a soft oath yanked it over her head. As if a floodgate had been opened, they began to tear at each other's clothes, tossing away the barriers between them with each piece of clothing.

When they were both naked from the waist up, he suddenly stopped. He stared down at her and with a sure hand cupped her breast in his palm. Then, with exquisite patience, he slid down along her body, his lips and hands branding a path as he moved from her shoulder to her breast, to her waist, to her backside.

Desire built inside her with every tender caress and she could think of nothing more than total surrender. And when he knelt in front of her, he finished the job he had begun, undressing her with great patience and restraint, his mouth exploring every inch of newly exposed flesh...her toes, her ankles, the curve of her calf and the soft skin of her inner thigh.

Perrie braced her hands on his shoulders, his muscles bunching and shifting beneath her fingers as he moved. And when she stood naked before him, she felt her pulse quicken and her breath disappear. There was no way to go back now, no thought of escape. For this moment, she belonged to Joe, utterly and entirely, without fear or regret.

He advanced again, across her belly, nibbling and kissing, moving lower and lower until his tongue penetrated the moist core of her desire. Her knees buckled and she cried out his name as wave after wave of pure sensation raced through her body. He eased her back on the bed, drawing his hand along the length of her, from neck to hip, the heat from his fingers marking her skin.

There was no other man for her, now or ever. After this night, she would never again feel this surge of passion or the power of his touch. She would grow old knowing that only one man had seen to the very depths of her soul, had driven all inhibition from her body, and had possessed her in the most intimate way.

With Joe, she had become a woman, not just in name, but in the very heart of her being. Beneath his touch, she came alive, transformed by the pleasure they took in each other. She arched against him, his hair soft between her fingers as his tongue continued to work its magic. Coherent thought slipped from her mind and all that remained was pure pleasure.

With each stroke, the tension in her core grew until she twisted beneath him, aching for her release. Again and again, he brought her close, but then drew her back from the edge with delicious care. Frustrated, she tugged at his hair, pulling him back, impatient with this game he played. "Enough," she said.

A lazy smile curled his mouth and he watched her

through half-hooded eyes. "What do you want? Tell me."

"I want you," Perrie said. "Inside of me."

He stood and skimmed his jeans and boxer shorts down over his hips, kicking them off with bare feet. Then he turned and rummaged through his duffel until he found a small foil package.

Biting her lower lip, she held out her hand and he placed the condom in her palm. Raising herself up to sit on the edge of the bed, she gazed at him, taking in the ripe beauty of his body, taut muscle and hard desire, a silken shaft of steel. With trembling fingers, she sheathed him, and then together, they tumbled back onto the soft bed.

He settled his hips between her legs and she closed her eyes and lost herself in the feel of their bodies, skin against skin. Smooth muscle met soft flesh, hard desire probed moist heat, and two bodies slowly became one.

Nothing had prepared her for the power of their coupling. As he drove inside of her, she lost all sense of reality and, instead, spun on a vortex of overwhelming pleasure. The blood burned in her veins and soft, incoherent cries escaped her throat with each thrust. Nerves tingled deep inside of her, and as he moved faster, the tension grew.

She wrapped her legs around his waist, and all at once she felt herself soar toward her release. Her muscles tensed and she stopped breathing, and then it came, surging through her and pooling at the place where they were joined. He cried out at the same time and she dug her nails into his back as he gave himself over to her.

She lost all sense of time. Seconds were marked by heartbeats and minutes by soft gasps for breath. As they drifted back to reality, her thoughts cleared and she felt a warm sense of contentment. This was her reality now. She had loved a man as she had loved no other. Later, in the dark of night, she could think about all that she was going to lose. But for now, she and Joe were together.

She waited for him to say something, but he didn't. He just pulled her into the curve of his body and wrapped his arms around her, so tight that she wondered how he'd ever let her go.

It was as if he were waiting for her to speak, to tell him what she felt. Perrie closed her eyes and slowed her breathing, pretending to sleep in the hopes that she might stave off any passionate declarations. But that was not to be, for a long while later, in the silence of the night, Joe drew her closer.

"I love you, Perrie," he murmured, his warm lips pressed against her shoulder. "And I know you love me."

Hours later, long after Joe had drifted into sleep, Perrie still lay awake. Though morning approached, the room was dark. She slipped out of bed and gathered her clothes, then silently dressed. No matter how hard she tried, she couldn't draw her gaze away from him. He looked so sweet, so vulnerable, the sheets twisted through his limbs, his hair mussed.

But this was all a dream. That's what she had to keep reminding herself. For the past two weeks, she'd lived someone else's life, a woman she barely knew. With a man she barely knew. She couldn't change the rest of her life just because she had let herself get lost in a fantasy for a short time.

With all the courage she possessed, Perrie took one last look at Joe, then turned and walked to the door. Everything would be all right. She would be able to put this all behind her once she got back to Seattle.

10

WHEN JOE WOKE UP the next morning, she was gone. He had almost expected her to stay. But then, what had passed between them probably had meant even less to her than he had imagined. Like a fool, he had waited around at the resort until noon, hoping that she would return. But by then she was halfway to Seattle, and he knew the odds were not in his favor.

He'd seen the last of Perrie Kincaid. In a few days she'd be happily back in the midst of Seattle's underworld, chasing wise guys and dodging bullets. Hell, how could he blame her? Muleshoe must have seemed as dull as dust in comparison. Spaghetti feeds, dogsled races, endless cold and snow. There were times when the place drove him a little crazy, too.

He had packed his bags and left for the small airstrip on the west side of Cooper shortly after noon. As soon as he'd gotten up in the air, he'd turned the plane toward Muleshoe. But he'd known there would be no relief at home, for everywhere he'd turned he would see Perrie—in her cabin, with the dogs, trudging through the woods on a pair of old snowshoes. And later, when he finally put an end to this day, when he lay in bed alone, he would see her in different ways, naked in his arms, her body flushed with passion, her eyes filled with need.

The fire snapped, sending a shower of sparks over the hearth and bringing Joe back to the present. He slouched down on the sofa and turned his attention to his flight log. Now that he was back at the lodge, the reminders seemed almost overwhelming. Nothing he did could put her out of his head.

He had been a fool to fall in love with her. In all the time he'd lived in Alaska, he'd never once allowed himself to need a woman. And then Perrie was dropped on his doorstep, and within days he'd fallen, and fallen hard. Yet through it all, he'd ignored one basic fact. She never wanted to be in Alaska. Perrie Kincaid belonged in Seattle.

Odd how the cards fell. Until five years ago, Joe had lived in the same city, had driven on the same streets and dined at the same restaurants. And then he had decided to change his life, to look for new adventures in the Alaskan wilderness. Only to fall in love with a woman from a life he'd left behind.

"Hey, what are you doing back here? I thought you and Perrie were spending the weekend at the Hot Springs."

Joe twisted on the sofa and saw Tanner standing in the middle of the great room, a power drill in his hand. "Well, things don't always go as planned."

Tanner crossed the room and sat down on the end of the coffee table. "Is she gone?"

Joe nodded.

"You told her about her boss's call?"

A cynical chuckle was all he could manage. "I didn't have to. She left on her own. Hired a pilot within an hour of our arrival at Cooper and then took off the next morning. No goodbyes, no 'see you soon,' nothing."

Tanner sighed and rubbed his palms on his knees. "Hey, buddy, I'm sorry."

The flight log snapped shut and Joe straightened.

"Well, don't be. I should have known better. I mean, it's not like she chose to come up here. She was forced into it."

"And she didn't choose to fall in love with you?"

"She wasn't in love with me," Joe replied, shaking his head. "If she were, she would have stayed."

"Not necessarily. Julia didn't."

"Julia's different. She's not as…difficult."

Tanner laughed. "You don't know the half of it, Brennan."

"There just wasn't much chance for Perrie and me. I should have realized that, but I got caught up in something neither one of us really thought out."

"So, you're just going to let it go?"

Joe considered Tanner's question for a long moment, then nodded once. "Yep." He got up from the sofa and gathered the papers he'd spread around him on the cushions. "I've got to make a run up to Fort Yukon. I think I'll spend the night there."

"What if she calls?" Tanner asked.

"She won't call." Joe grabbed his jacket from the back of the sofa, tucked the flight log under his arm and headed for the door.

When he reached the solitude of the outdoors, he drew a deep breath and looked up at the sky. But against his will, his gaze was drawn to Perrie's cabin. A vision of her flashed in his mind and he pushed it aside with a soft oath. He needed to get back up in the air. Once he was flying, he could clear his thoughts.

But something pulled him toward her cabin and he slowly trudged up the hill, knowing that he'd only revive more memories. He stopped once at the bottom of the steps, then continued to the door and walked inside.

The cabin was just as she'd left it. Julia hadn't known

that Perrie wasn't returning, so she hadn't called Edna to clean it. He crossed to the kitchen and picked up a coffee mug, running his fingers over the handle as if he might still feel the warmth of her hand, but it was as cold as the air that filled the room.

He set the cup down, then wandered over to the bed. The pillow still smelled of her shampoo, sweet and fruity. He could almost feel her hair between his fingers, silken strands of fiery auburn. And they'd slept in this bed just two nights ago and— Joe cursed softly. Was it necessary to torture himself? There were plenty of regrets to go around. He didn't have to dredge them up.

"I have to get out of here," he muttered, throwing the pillow back on the bed.

He strode from the cabin and headed toward the shed. As requested, Burdy had loaded five crates of building supplies into the back of the pickup, supplies that had been delivered from Fairbanks by another bush pilot. Joe had planned to fly them up to Fort Yukon after he and Perrie returned from Cooper Hot Springs. But now he could make his delivery early and have an excuse to get away from the lodge.

Hell, maybe he'd just keep flying, hopping from airstrip to airstrip until he managed to purge Perrie Kincaid from his head. He'd go south or east. Maybe he'd find a warm place, an island somewhere, with beautiful women and endless bottles of rum. Or he could fly to a city and lose himself in the midst of crowds of people and concrete buildings.

Joe jumped in the truck and started the engine, then carefully wove through the trees on the narrow, snow-packed drive. He sped through Muleshoe and headed out of town for the airstrip, ignoring the flood of memories that came with each familiar landmark in town.

The Super Cub was still warm from his trip back from Cooper. He loaded the crates, then glanced at his watch. He had plenty of time to make Fort Yukon before dark.

He steered the Cub out onto the runway and increased the throttle. The plane took off in an instant, lifting up into the air before he'd covered half the airstrip. Joe closed his eyes as he climbed into the sky, the whine of the plane's ascent like a balm to his nerves.

He banked north, the wilderness spreading out in front of him. He could lose himself in Alaska as easily as he could lose himself anywhere else. And if he flew far enough and high enough and long enough, maybe then he'd forget her.

PERRIE STARED at her computer screen, watching the cursor blink until her eyes began to cross. She shook her head and rubbed her eyes with her fingertips. Maybe she should have stayed at home instead of coming in to the office. She'd left Alaska at sunrise and it was now nearly eight in the evening. But she'd been away for so long. The sooner she got back into her daily routine, the sooner she could put the last two weeks behind her.

Besides, she had to finish the brides story. It hung over her like a dark cloud, filled with flashes of memory and rumblings of regret. She couldn't think of her time in Muleshoe without thinking of him—and all they'd shared. And the brides story was part of that.

Him. Maybe if she didn't call him by name, he wouldn't seem so real. Perhaps she could learn to look at Joe Brennan as nothing more than a brief passage in her life, a vague remembrance, part of a story she'd soon put to bed.

But no matter how hard she tried, Joe refused to become anything less than a living, breathing man who intruded on her thoughts again and again. The memories were so vivid and so alive that she could still feel his skin beneath her palms, still taste his mouth against hers, still hear his soft moans in her—

"Kincaid! You're back."

Blinking hard, Perrie snapped herself out of the daydream, almost thankful for the distraction. She straightened in her chair, mentally steeling herself for one of Milt Freeman's rants. Her editor would not be happy to see her, but he'd have to deal with it. There was no way she'd let him send her back to Alaska. She was here and she planned to stay.

Perrie turned to smile at him, but to her surprise, he seemed genuinely happy to see her. Where was the man who demanded that she be banished to the wilderness? Where was the man so set on protecting her? "I am back, Milt."

He patted her on the shoulder. "Ah, Kincaid. I've missed you. I thought you'd be back sooner."

"Well, I would have. But I was stuck in Muleshoe, thanks to you. I tried to leave. Unfortunately, your pal Joe Brennan made sure there was no way out of town."

"Good man, that Brennan. I knew I could trust him with the job."

"He got the job done, all right," she said.

"When I called the other day, Joe's partner said you two were out. So, you and Brennan got along?"

"Yeah, we got along." The last person she wanted to blather on about was Brennan. It was bad enough that her thoughts were filled with him. She didn't need Milt bringing his name up in conversation every— Perrie frowned. "You called the lodge?"

"Yeah. Evening before last. The FBI arrested Riordan and Dearborn. Case against them is solid. I thought you'd be here yesterday so we could get your piece in the Monday morning edition. I had to have Landers write the initial story. By the way, where is all your research? I went through your—"

"They got Riordan and Dearborn? But how could they? I took all my evidence with me."

"They're the FBI, Kincaid. They specialize in catching crooks and they had all kinds of evidence of their own. They've been on to Dearborn longer than you have. And once you were safely out of the way, they could finally do their job."

Perrie frowned. "If you hadn't sent me to Muleshoe, I would have broken that story. I was..." She paused. "You called the lodge on Saturday evening?"

"Isn't that what I said?"

"What exactly did you tell them?"

"I said it was all right for you to come back. O'Neill said he'd let Brennan or you know right away. I figured you'd have Brennan fly you out the minute you heard. So where the hell were you? And when can I have your story?"

Perrie's mind raced. Joe must have known it was all right for her to go home to Seattle. After they'd returned from the Muleshoe Games, he had stopped at the lodge. Had Tanner given him the message then? And if he had, why hadn't Joe passed it along to her?

A single thought raced through her mind. Had he *wanted* her to stay? Perrie buried her face in her hands and rubbed her tired eyes again, trying to make some sense of the situation.

Since she'd left Alaska, something had been niggling at her brain, but she hadn't been able to put it into words. Now it suddenly became clear. He hadn't told her that she could leave. And when she had left, he hadn't even tried to stop her. In fact, he'd almost opened the door and let her go. He'd known it was all right for her to return; he'd known since they'd slept together the night before.

"He just wanted to have sex!" she cried, not realizing until too late that she'd spoken out loud.

"Who wanted to have sex?"

Perrie shook her head and waved distractedly at Milt. Brennan had kept the news from her deliberately. She frowned. But then, she'd been the one to show up at his door. Had she stayed in her own room, they never would have made love that night at the resort.

Love. The word rang in Perrie's head. He had said the words while she had pretended to be asleep. *I love you, Perrie, and I know you love me.* At the time, she'd brushed them off, thinking that they were empty of meaning outside the bedroom.

But what if Brennan was speaking from his heart? What if he truly loved her? "But if he loved me, why did he let me leave?" she said.

"Kincaid, what the hell are you mumbling about?"

Perrie glanced up at Milt, then shook her head and groaned. "I'm so confused. And I think I may have made a big mistake."

"On the Riordan story?"

"Oh, to hell with the Riordan story, Milt. I'm talking about me and Joe. I just walked out on him. When, all the while, he believed I would want to stay."

"Stay where?"

"In Alaska."

Milt stared at her, head cocked, as if she'd completely lost her mind. Then he patted her on the shoulder again. "By the way, I showed your wolf story around. Great piece of work. In fact, one of the syndicates got hold of it and called me. Wanted to pay big bucks for more. I told him you didn't live in Alaska and there wouldn't be more."

"I could live in Alaska," Perrie said, the notion not nearly as ridiculous as it once seemed.

"No, you couldn't," Milt replied. "You work in Seattle."

"I wouldn't have to work in Seattle. I could work in Muleshoe. I could call that syndicator and sell my stories to him. I have a lot more. And I could string for the Fairbanks or Anchorage paper. Or I could start my own paper. There's this old newspaper office above Paddy Doyle's tavern. I mean, I'd have to upgrade the equipment, get a computer, maybe even a new press. And there's not much circulation. But Joe makes flights into the bush all the time. I bet those families would be glad to get some local news. And running a weekly would be—"

"Kincaid! Stop! You're talking like a crazy woman. You can't live in Alaska."

A slow smile grew on Perrie's lips. "Yes, I can. I can live wherever I want."

"But what about your career?"

"I'm a writer, Milt. I can write anywhere, including Muleshoe, Alaska."

"I think you're overtired, Kincaid. Jet-lagged. Maybe you've been in the wilderness too long. It's my fault. I made a mistake sending you there. Go home. Get some rest. You can write the Riordan story tomorrow."

Perrie reached down beneath the desk and grabbed the strap of her shoulder bag, then yanked it out. "No, Milt," she said, placing the bag in his arms. "You can write the Riordan story. Here are all my notes and research and evidence."

"The story is yours, Kincaid. You have to write it."

She stood up. "No, I don't. Right now, I have to go back to Alaska. I have to find out if Joe Brennan really loves me."

"Joe Brennan loves you? My Joe Brennan?"

Perrie laughed. "He *was* your Joe Brennan, but now he's *my* Joe Brennan." She grabbed the phone from the corner of the desk. "I have to call him and tell him I'm coming." She snatched her hand away. "No, maybe I should just fly up there and talk to him." She shook her head. "I'll call Julia. I'll let her know I'm coming. She can pick me up at the airstrip."

Perrie rummaged through the bag Milt held, searching for her day planner before she realized she didn't have the number for the lodge. "I need the phone number. Get me the phone number, Milt. Never mind, I'll get it."

She sprang out of her chair and hurried toward Milt's office. His phone file was on his desk and she riffled through it until she found the card for the Bachelor Creek Lodge. Grabbing Milt's chair, she pulled it up to the desk and sat down, then dialed the phone.

Her heart pounded in her chest and she prayed that Joe wouldn't answer. When she finally spoke to him again, she wanted to be standing face-to-face. She wanted to be able to look into his eyes and see the truth there.

The phone was answered on the first ring. "Joe?" said a feminine voice.

"Julia?"

"Who is this?"

Perrie cleared her throat. "It's Perrie Kincaid."

"Oh, Perrie. Thank goodness you called. Has Joe contacted you?"

Perrie frowned. "No, he hasn't. Isn't he there?"

A long silence met her question. Then Julia finally spoke. "Perrie, I have some bad news. Joe was ferrying supplies to a town near the Arctic Circle and he never showed up. He filed a flight plan and he radioed ahead so they were expecting him before dark. He took the Cub. At first we thought he might have flown down to see you."

"Me?"

"Tanner said he seemed pretty upset after you left. We thought he might have flown down to Seattle to straighten things out."

"He—he isn't here," Perrie said. "He didn't call."

"Hawk says that Joe would never deliberately deviate from his flight plan. That's why we're worried."

"He's a good pilot," Perrie murmured. "The best. He'd never..." Her heart turned to ice and her breath froze in her chest as the true meaning of Julia's words sank in. Joe's plane had gone down in the wilderness and they didn't know where he was.

She brought her fingers to her mouth to stop a cry of fear, then blinked back the sudden flood of tears pressing at the corners of her eyes.

"I'm flying up there," Perrie said, her voice surprisingly calm. "I'll get a flight out as soon as I can. I may have to fly into Anchorage and then on to Fairbanks, but I'll get there by morning. I promise."

"Perrie, you don't have to—"

"I want to be there, Julia. I belong in Muleshoe."

"All right. Call the lodge before you leave Fairbanks and I'll send Hawk out to the airstrip to pick you up."

"I'll be there as soon as I can. And, Julia?"

"Yes?"

"If they find him before I get there, would you tell him that I love him? And that everything will work out?"

THE TINY AIRSTRIP at Muleshoe appeared in the distance just as the sun was rising. Perrie stared out the window of the bush plane, shielding her eyes against the glare, hoping she might see the red wings of Joe's Super Cub. But as the pilot descended, her heart fell, as well. There was no sign of the plane.

She said a silent prayer, hoping that Joe had turned up at another airstrip, hoping that he was safe in some other bush town. She'd been in the air all night, flying from Seattle to Anchorage to Fairbanks. And then she had struggled to find a bush pilot in the early hours of the morning.

They'd left Fairbanks before dawn, and as they came into Muleshoe, she realized that she hadn't slept in more than two days, since the last night she and Joe had spent together at her cabin. Her thoughts skipped back to that night, and then to the night after, when they'd made love.

She couldn't allow herself to believe that they would never see each other again. Joe had to be alive and safe. He flew in the wilderness all the time and he had bragged that he could put the Cub down anywhere he pleased. If he'd had trouble, perhaps he'd safely landed the plane and was just waiting to be found.

"Looks like there's someone down there," the pilot shouted, pointing to the far end of the runway.

Perrie squinted against the rising sun and saw the Blazer parked near the row of planes. As the pilot circled the landing strip, she caught sight of Hawk, staring up into the sky. She had talked to him by phone right before she'd left Fairbanks and there had been no news of Joe.

Now, two hours later, she wondered if anything had changed.

The plane landed on the smooth snow and slid to a stop. Perrie shoved the door open and hopped out, then ran across the snow toward Hawk. She threw herself into his arms and he hugged her tight, picking her up off the ground. Then he set her down and stepped back. "I'm glad you came."

"Has there been any news?"

Hawk shook his head. "They're sending out search planes right now. We'll find him."

"What about his radio? Hasn't he tried to contact anyone?"

"Maybe his radio is out."

"But how could the radio just go out, unless—" Perrie stopped short, not wanting to complete the thought. Unless the plane was damaged. Unless Joe had crashed somewhere in the wilderness.

"There are lots of reasons he could have lost radio contact," Hawk assured her. "If he put down in a valley, the mountains might block the signal."

"You know the route he was flying, don't you? So the search teams can find him more quickly?"

"He was flying up to Fort Yukon. He never—"

"Fort Yukon?" Perrie asked. "He was going to Fort Yukon?"

"He was taking supplies up there. He has survival gear in the plane. Sleeping bags and dried food. So if he had to put her down, he would be able to wait for us to find him."

A sudden thought came to Perrie's mind when Hawk mentioned sleeping bags. "I think I might know where he is," she said. "What if he put the plane down for a reason, then couldn't take off again?"

"Why would he put the plane down?"

"Maybe he stopped to see Romeo and Juliet," Perrie replied.

"The play?"

"No, the wolves," she cried. "You know, the family of wolves that he watches up at the Yukon Flats. He took me to see them."

"Joe visits a family of wolves?" Hawk seemed completely taken aback by the revelation. "Can you remember where you landed up there?"

"We were at the Gebhardts' cabin."

"On Van Hatten Creek?"

Perrie nodded. "And then we flew west, I think. I didn't notice at first, but then the landscape looked so different from Muleshoe. There was a huge mountain out the left window and I remember the sun was shining off the snow. There were no trees on it."

"That was probably Snowy Peak."

"Then I think we turned north again, out of the sun. There were lots of trees below and mountains. But then the landscape kind of cleared and there was a wide area that was just snow. It was really flat, like a river covered in white. And that's where Joe put the plane down. He said we were on the southern edge of the wildlife refuge."

"Was there another peak? You should have seen it to the east. Bear Mountain."

Perrie bit her lower lip and tried to remember, but once they'd landed, she had lost her sense of direction. Her attention had been focused on the wolves and on Joe, not on the surrounding mountains. "I don't know," she said in a shaky voice. "Maybe there was. I'd know the landscape if I saw it. I remember that peak."

The pilot from the bush plane walked over toward

them, Perrie's bags in his arms. "Here are your things, ma'am."

Perrie grabbed his arm. "How much fuel do you have left in your plane?"

"Enough to get me back to Fairbanks."

"Enough to fly up to Fort Yukon?"

Hawk picked up on her idea. "Never mind about the fuel. We can fill the plane up here. I need you to fly me up to Yukon Flats."

"Me, too!" Perrie cried. "I'm coming along."

The pilot shook his head. "But I've got to get back to—"

"This is a search and rescue," Hawk explained.

The pilot's expression immediately turned from indifference to concern. "Who are we looking for?"

"Joe Brennan."

"Polar Bear Air? I know Brennan."

"We think he might have put the plane down on purpose somewhere up on the flats yesterday."

The pilot grabbed Perrie's bags and tossed them inside the Blazer. "Then let's refuel and get up in the air. Maybe we can find him before he has to spend another night in the cold."

Hawk nodded, then grabbed Perrie's hand and gave it a squeeze. "We'll find him."

The next fifteen minutes passed in a flurry of activity. Hawk helped the pilot refuel, then he called the lodge on the plane's radio just as they were taking off to let Tanner know their plans. They were up in the air before Perrie had a chance to grow impatient.

"He went to see Romeo," she murmured. "I know he did."

She stared out the window from her place behind the pilot's seat, trying to remember the landscape that she'd watched so closely that day. When they reached the spot above the Gebhardts' cabin, she sat up straighter, hoping that Joe's plane might be sitting out front. But Perrie saw nothing there except snow and a thin curl of smoke from the chimney.

The pilot veered west and Snowy Peak appeared in her window. "This is right," she called. "We took off in this direction. We were just about even with the peak when Joe turned north again."

The pilot waited until the plane drew closer to the mountain, then banked to the right. Below them, the landscape looked unfamiliar and Perrie's heart twisted. "This isn't right," she said. "I don't recognize this."

"Just wait," Hawk called from the copilot's seat. "I think Joe might have followed the Little Black River north. Before too long it meets Paddle Creek and there's a wide flat area right near the edge of the refuge."

She took a deep breath and pressed her palm to her heart, trying to calm the rapid pounding in her chest. She felt the crunch of paper beneath her jacket, then reached inside and withdrew the valentine Joe had made for her. Throughout her trip back to Muleshoe, it had rested near her heart, a reminder of what they had shared. She stared at it now, as if willing some mystical power from the paper and lace.

She wasn't sure how long she looked at it, rubbing her fingers over Joe's casual scrawl, remembering the day he'd given it to her.

"Well, I'll be damned."

Perrie looked up to see Hawk staring out his window, a pair of binoculars pressed to his eyes. "What? Do you see something?"

Hawk slowly lowered the binoculars then turned and

smiled at Perrie. "You were right. He's down there. And the plane looks like it's in one piece."

Perrie scrambled to the window on the other side of the plane. In the distance she could see a splash of red against the white snow. "Is he all right? Can you see him?"

Hawk looked down again and nodded. "He sees us. He's waving."

Perrie leaned back in her seat and closed her eyes. A surge of relief, followed by apprehension rushed over her and suddenly she wasn't sure of what she'd planned. What if she'd been mistaken? What if Joe didn't love her the way she thought he did?

"I'm going to put her down," the pilot called.

"Are—are you sure?" Perrie asked. "I—I mean, someone else could rescue him. You've already done so much."

Hawk turned and looked at her. "He'll be happy to see you."

His words were so direct and so confident that Perrie couldn't help but believe him. She smiled, then mouthed a silent "thank you" to the man who had become such a good friend.

The pilot circled once, but Perrie was afraid to look down. Her entire life, her happiness were riding on this landing. On the hope that she was right about Joe and that he truly did love her. The hope that he wanted her to come back to him, that there was a place in his life for her.

Moments later the plane was on the ground, and they slid across the snow until the pilot pulled back on the throttle and they came to a stop. Through the window, Perrie watched as Joe ran toward the plane, but she was frozen in her seat, unable to move.

Hawk hopped out and ran toward him, then grabbed Joe around the neck and gave him a hug. They talked for a minute, their heads bent, and then Hawk looked back to the plane. Perrie said one more prayer, pushed the door open and stepped outside.

But as she left the shadow of the plane's wing, Joe turned and started back toward the Super Cub. She stepped into the sunshine and Hawk called to Joe. He turned back, a grin on his face. And then he saw her.

Perrie held her breath, her fingers clutching at the valentine in her hands. His grin gradually faded to an expression of confusion and then disbelief. He pushed his cap off and ran his hand through his hair, then shook his head.

Their gazes locked, and, finally, after what seemed to Perrie like an eternity, he slowly started toward her. With each step his smile grew, along with the relief she felt. He stopped, then laughed out loud and held out his arms. Perrie gave a little cry and raced toward him.

She threw herself into his embrace, so hard that they both nearly fell back into the snow. His fingers furrowed through her hair and he brought his mouth down on hers, kissing her wildly, frantically, joyously. "I thought I'd never see you again," he murmured against her lips. "What are you doing here?"

"I had to come back," Perrie replied, trailing a line of kisses along his jaw. "I had to tell you."

"To tell me why you left?"

"No, I had to tell you why I have to stay." She looked up into the brilliant blue of his eyes. "I love you, Joe Brennan."

He stared at her a long moment, then glanced up at the sky and smiled. "You had better love me, Kincaid," he said, looking back down at her. "Because I sure as hell love you."

With a shout of delight, Perrie wrapped her arms around his neck and kissed him hard. "Do you know how scared I was? When I called the lodge and they told me your plane was missing, I didn't know what to do."

"I stopped to see Romeo and Juliet," Joe said. "I stayed a little too long and when I tried to take off, I couldn't get any power. Ice in the fuel line. By the time I figured that out, it was too dark to see to fix it. I just got it cleared when I saw your plane."

Perrie held his face between her palms. "Why didn't you use the radio and call someone?"

"I did. I radioed Fort Yukon but I couldn't raise anyone on that end. So I radioed the lodge and left my location with Sammy. I explained that he was supposed to have Tanner call Fort Yukon for me and tell them I'd be there in the morning."

"Sammy didn't say a thing."

"Hawk told me that after Fort Yukon reported me late, Julia sent Sam off with Burdy, knowing that he'd be upset if he knew I was missing. They didn't explain the situation to him. And Sam just forgot to mention that he'd talked to me."

"I was so worried. I thought I'd lost you."

"Why did you leave me, Perrie? Why did you just walk away?"

She pressed her forehead into his chest, unable to meet his gaze. "Because I was stupid and scared and I didn't believe that you really loved me. I just thought you were doing your job, doing what Milt wanted you to do."

Joe chuckled and tipped her chin up. "Milt never mentioned anything about falling in love with you."

"I meant sleeping with me."

"He didn't mention that, either. I thought of that all on my own."

Perrie felt a warm blush creep up her cheeks. "We are good together."

"Yes, Kincaid, we do make quite a pair," he teased. "And since you agree, I suppose there's only one thing left to do."

Perrie gave him a coy look, as anxious as he was to return to the lodge and a nice warm bed. She felt as if she could sleep, and make love to him, for the next week. "And what's that, Brennan?"

"You'll have to marry me."

She gasped, his words taking her breath away. When it finally returned, she cleared her throat. "Marry you?"

"Just say yes, sweetheart. We'll figure out where we're going to live and what we're going to do later. Right now, all I need to know is that you'll spend the rest of your life with me."

With a shout of delight, she launched herself into his arms again, this time knocking them both down into the snow. They rolled over and over each other, kissing and laughing until Joe pinned her arms over her head and lay on top of her.

"So will you?" he asked.

"Yes, yes, yes. But only if we can live in Muleshoe," Perrie replied.

Joe blinked in surprise. "Really. You want to live in Alaska?"

Perrie nodded and Joe pressed her face between his palms and kissed her, long and deep. Then he looked up and smiled, his gaze fixed on the far horizon. "We're being watched," he said, rolling off her.

Perrie turned onto her stomach and braced her elbows

in the snow. Across the wide expanse of flat land, she saw a movement, a flash of gray against a background of white. Romeo came into view and, a few seconds later, Juliet appeared.

Joe put his arm around Perrie's waist, then leaned over and kissed her on the temple. "Do you think they approve?" he asked.

"Every lone wolf deserves a mate," Perrie said. "And now you've found yours."

With a low growl, Joe pulled her into his arms, and, in that moment, Perrie knew she'd found her place in the wilderness. She'd found her soul mate. And together, they'd make a life for each other.

THE MEN OF BACHELOR CREEK

Alaska. A place where men could be men—and women were scarce!

To Tanner, Joe and Hawk, Alaska was the final frontier. They'd gone to the ends of the earth to flee the one thing they all feared—MATRIMONY. Little did they know that three intrepid heroines would brave the wilds to "save" them from their lonely bachelor existences.

Enjoy

#662 CAUGHT UNDER THE MISTLETOE!
December 1997

#670 DODGING CUPID'S ARROW!
February 1998

#678 STRUCK BY SPRING FEVER!
April 1998

by Kate Hoffmann

Available wherever Harlequin books are sold.

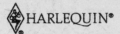 HARLEQUIN®

Not The Same Old Story!

 HARLEQUIN PRESENTS®

Exciting, glamorous romance stories that take readers around the world.

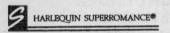 Harlequin Romance®

Sparkling, fresh and tender love stories that bring you pure romance.

HARLEQUIN® *Temptation.*

Bold and adventurous— Temptation is strong women, bad boys, great sex!

HARLEQUIN SUPERROMANCE®

Provocative and realistic stories that celebrate life and love.

 HARLEQUIN® AMERICAN ◆ ROMANCE®

Contemporary fairy tales—where anything is possible and where dreams come true.

HARLEQUIN® INTRIGUE®

Heart-stopping, suspenseful adventures that combine the best of romance and mystery.

 LOVE & LAUGHTER™

Humorous and romantic stories that capture the lighter side of love.

Look us up on-line at: http://www.romance.net   HGENERIC

It's a dating wasteland out there! So what's
a girl to do when there's not a marriage-
minded man in sight? Go hunting, of course.

Enjoy the hilarious antics of five intrepid heroines,
determined to lead Mr. Right to the altar—
whether he wants to go or not!

She's got a plan—to find herself a man!

Available wherever Harlequin books are sold.

**It's hot...
and it's out of control!**

**It's a two-alarm Blaze—
from one of Temptation's newest authors!**

This spring, Temptation turns up the heat. Look
for these bold, provocative, *ultra*-sexy books!

#679 PRIVATE PLEASURES
Janelle Denison
April 1998

Mariah Stevens wanted a husband. Grey Nichols
wanted a lover. But Mariah was determined.
For better or worse, there would be no more private
pleasures for Grey without a public ceremony.

#682 PRIVATE FANTASIES
Janelle Denison
May 1998

For Jade Stevens, Kyle was the man of her dreams. He
seemed to know her every desire—in bed and out. Little
did she know that he'd come across her book of private
fantasies—or that he intended to make every one come true!

BLAZE! Red-hot reads from Temptation!

HARLEQUIN®

Temptation.

DEBBIE MACOMBER

invites you to the

★ ♥ HEART OF TEXAS ★

Join Debbie Macomber as she brings you the lives and loves of the folks in the ranching community of Promise, Texas.

If you loved Midnight Sons—don't miss Heart of Texas! A brand-new six-book series from Debbie Macomber.

Available in February 1998 at your favorite retail store.

Heart of Texas by Debbie Macomber

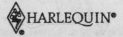 HARLEQUIN®

KEY TO MY HEART

Unlock the secrets of romance just in time for the most romantic day of the year— Valentine's Day!

Key to My Heart
features three of your favorite authors,

Kasey Michaels,
Rebecca York
and Muriel Jensen,

to bring you wonderful tales of romance and Valentine's Day dreams come true.

As an added bonus you can receive Harlequin's special Valentine's Day necklace. FREE with the purchase of every *Key to My Heart* collection.

Available in January,
wherever Harlequin books are sold.

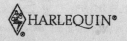

**Look for these titles—
available at your favorite retail outlet!**

January 1998
Renegade Son by Lisa Jackson

Danielle Summers had problems: a rebellious child
and unscrupulous enemies. In addition, her Montana
ranch was slowly being sabotaged. And then there was
Chase McEnroe—who admired her land and desired her
body. But Danielle feared he would invade more than just
her property—he'd trespass on her heart.

February 1998
The Heart's Yearning by Ginna Gray

Fourteen years ago Laura gave her baby up for adoption,
and not one day had passed that she didn't think about
him and agonize over her choice—so she finally followed
her heart to Texas to see her child. But the plan to watch
her son from afar doesn't quite happen that way, once the
boy's sexy—*single*—father takes a decided interest in *her*.

March 1998
First Things Last by Dixie Browning

One look into Chandler Harrington's dark eyes and
Belinda Massey could refuse the Virginia millionaire nothing.
So how could the no-nonsense nanny believe the rumors that
he had kidnapped his nephew—an adorable, healthy little boy
who crawled as easily into her heart as he did into her lap?

**BORN IN THE USA: Love, marriage—
and the pursuit of family!**

Look us up on-line at: http://www.romance.net   BUSA4